Rane's Mate

by

Hazel Gower

Rane's Mate

ISBN: 978-1-940744-04-9
Edited by Pamela Tyner
Cover Art by Live Love Media

Published in the United States of America by Beachwalk Press, Incorporated

www.beachwalkpress.com

Dedication

To my best friend Kirby Beckley, I love you. Thank you for your support and for always being there for me. This book is for you. Also thanks to my awesome family.

Acknowledgements

Thank you to my amazing editor Pamela Tyner. I will be forever grateful you took a chance on me. Thank you to my writing friends, you know who you are.

Chapter 1

Rane was so sick of babysitting duty. Fine, he had fucked up, but it had been almost three months and Kane was still punishing him even though it had all worked out. Today's babysitting job was just plain cruel. Playing protector to four women at a place called The Big Day Out was going to be torture, especially with Faith, three and a half months pregnant. Kane wasn't happy about Faith going, but she had called it one of her 'normal person' days and argued that pregnant women went to concerts all the time. Kane had argued that if she had a vision and fell, she could hurt the baby. But Faith was having none of it; she was going, so Rane had been dragged into it.

Rane looked at Kane's house in front of him, remembering how he'd gotten talked into this new babysitting job.

"It's in the day, for most of the event, and my favorite bands are going to be there. Plus, I invited this woman from work who just moved here and hasn't got a lot of friends yet. For the last month and a half, she's been coming to my girls' day or nights out. We've started to become really good friends. She's such a sweetie, but do you want to know

the kicker? She's special, I just can't figure out what her ability is. I don't think she has visions, because I had a five minute one the other day and she showed no sign of knowing it." Faith didn't even pause when she turned to him and added, *"Rane will come with me, won't you?"*

She had blindsided him, changed the conversation so many times he got lost, so his answer became, "Err, sure, Faith. Argh, what am I saying sure to?"

His brother had laughed at him. "She's good, isn't she? Now that she's said it, I think it would set my mind at ease if you were there, and you do owe me and Faith."

Rane sighed and walked into the house. He found Kane and Bengie sitting on the lounge playing Mario Kart together.

Watching Kane as he cheered at Bengie for winning, then started a new game, Rane frowned, wondering why his brother wasn't going instead of him. "Why can't you take them, Kane?"

Kane didn't even look away from the game. "Because in an hour or so, I'm leaving to do rounds at the hospital. Plus, it's girls' day out." Kane laughed. "Sorry, brother, but her friends...don't get me wrong, I like them, but they're not fans of me. Well, I haven't met the new woman." He lowered his voice to barely a whisper. "I always thought they were a bad influence on her."

Rane stared at his brother, there was no way he was the only one going. Kane would never let his pregnant wife go to a major event without a whole heap of protection, even if that event was held partly in the day.

"You're way too calm. How many of us are going?"

"Only six, although Jamie, Devlin, and two others were already going to the concert, so really only two are going as back up." Rane turned his eyes heavenward, praying for patience.

"Shit! She doesn't know, does she? I hate you, Kane."

"She probably does, Faith's quick now with the psychic stuff."

"Fuck you, Kane. If she knew, you wouldn't still be whispering."

Kane laughed as Faith came in. "What's so funny, honey?" she asked.

Kane looked over at his mate. "I thought you were going to get ready. Where is the rest of your outfit?"

Faith rolled her eyes.

Rane had to admit, if only to himself, that she did look hot. Faith's hair was in a messy bun, and a pink lacy bra was peeking out of the top of her sparkling pink singlet. You would never know she was three and a half months pregnant with a werewolf baby. Faith had a tiny, miniscule bump for a baby tummy. He looked further down to see skintight short shorts, toned tanned legs, and gladiator sandals.

"You're game to let her go out looking like that, Kane? I would never let my mate out of the house looking like that. Ha! You said this would be an easy job. I'm going to be fighting off advances all day and night."

Kane growled and grabbed his mate around the waist, fastening his mouth on hers. Rane tried not to laugh, but it was so funny to rile Kane. Four months ago he wouldn't have growled at him or anyone. Kane had always been the calm, cool, collected brother.

Bengie groaned. "They're at it again. They're so gross." The doorbell rang and Bengie jumped up, running to the door. "Remy's here!"

Faith giggled. "Please tell me I wasn't that pathetic when I had a crush on you."

Rane laughed, remembering a time when Kane had come home from University and Faith had been helping his mum and sisters bake cookies. She had dropped her mixing spoon and ran to the door yelling, "My prince is here, my prince is here."

"Noooo, you were worse," he and Kane said together.

Remy and Sara came strolling in carrying bags, and poor Bengie looked weighed down with suitcases.

"Who's worse?" Remy asked, though her eyes never left Kane's. Boy, if looks could kill...

Rane decided to help his brother out. "Faith is. We were talking about how bad Faith used to be with Kane."

Faith groaned. "Shut up, Rane." She hid her face in Kane's shoulder.

"Let's just say that Prince Kane saved Faith from dragons a lot." Rane couldn't help the grin as he remembered the games they'd played.

"Really?" Sara said. "I thought Kane was a lot older, wouldn't he have been away?"

Faith groaned again. "Sara, shut up."

Rane laughed. "Yes, he is a lot older. That's why it's so funny."

"Oh, shut it, Rane. You could never say no to me either. I seem to remember a time or two when you would be the wicked wit—"

"Okay, I think they get it now, Faith," Rane said quickly He looked around, eager for a subject change. "Are you girls moving in?"

When Kane paled, Rane couldn't hold in the chuckle.

"No, but we are going to stay for Faith's birthday

weekend," Remy said.

"And you needed all of this?"

Sara smiled. "I thought you said he has sisters, Faith?"

"He does but…" Faith stopped. "Kirby's here, but something's wrong." She looked at Kane. "Do you guys smell anything?"

Rane took a deep breath. His wolf sat up, but he didn't feel any danger. Moving to the door, Kane behind him, he took another deep breath. His wolf was wide awake, panting.

"I don't smell anything," Kane said. "What are you growling about?"

Rane shook himself as he opened the door, only to be pushed out of the way by Faith.

* * * *

Kirby was surrounded by wolves. They were everywhere in this town. Maybe she had finally gone crazy. Werewolves didn't exist. They were make believe, made up things you only found in scary movies. She'd had this feeling before but had ignored it, because it was only a person here or there. This time was bad. Kirby had an affinity for animals, she could kind of talk to them, and feel them. This feeling, however, was different.

Kirby opened her car door again, then shut it. She'd

feel bad if she left though, because she'd be bailing on Faith's birthday weekend, and Kirby was so looking forward to going to the big day out. Being independent and discovering new things on her own was one of the reasons she'd moved away from her overbearing, overprotective family. Kirby sighed. Her brothers were not there to save her or protect her in the event the wolves weren't so friendly.

The front door burst open, and Faith pushed past the hottest man Kirby had ever seen in her life. He was probably Faith's husband. He was gorgeous—short, wavy brown hair, six three, maybe six four, and all muscle. As he got closer to the car she could see his eyes were an electric blue, and he had a sharp nose that hovered over his lips. Kirby gulped and squeezed her legs shut. She could feel he was a werewolf, an alpha wolf, and he was looking at her like prey.

Kirby locked the doors. Faith's eyebrows drew together and her mouth turned down in a frown as she turned to the gorgeous werewolf and punched him in the chest, yelling something at him. Then she shook the hand she had used to hit the werewolf. Another taller werewolf came out and grabbed the first one. This one was beautiful too, but not the same as the other. The second werewolf came over and kissed Faith's hand, then went to the first werewolf, pulling him back a couple of steps.

Faith came over to the car. Kirby slowly unlocked the door and opened it.

"Kirby, what's wrong? Rane didn't mean to scare you. He's really a big softy."

Kirby looked all around her before she whispered, "I'm going crazy. I've never had it this strong before." Looking up, straight into Faith's eyes, she continued. "We're surrounded by werewolves, they're everywhere in this town." She was so freaked out she yelled the last part.

Faith winced, muttering under her breath. "It's this pregnancy that's making me miss stuff. I'm an idiot." Faith took Kirby's hands in hers, looked her in the eyes, and spoke clear this time. "You're an animal element or sensory, and I'm an idiot. I'm so sorry. I'm usually better at picking up these things, but I swear this pregnancy is putting me off. Kirby, I'm psychic, and a bunch of other things, but we'll keep to that one for now. No, you're not crazy, we are surrounded by werewolves, but they're good. They would never hurt you, and I'm not just saying that because I live with and mated one…well, us humans call it married. If you don't believe me, check for yourself. Tell me, what do you feel?"

Kirby took a step out of the car, closed her eyes, and tried to feel. She knew there were two werewolves near the house, but she felt no malice, or any desire to do her any harm. Kirby could feel two more in wolf form in the bushes, not far away, close enough that she tried to communicate with them. They didn't respond to her mind contact, though she did feel confusion from them and curiosity. Kirby did feel happy thoughts that she was there. Opening her eyes, she took another small step.

"Look, would it help if you saw one, got to touch a wolf? I promise you they won't hurt you." Nodding hesitantly, Faith yelled, "Blake, come here to us, slowly."

A beautiful, large black wolf with gray eyes ran out of the woods. He slowed a couple of feet away from them.

Faith walked up to him and looked over at Kirby as she said, "Okay, you're going to hear some growling, but just ignore it. I do. It won't be from Blake here."

Kirby placed her hand on Blake's furred covered body, running it up and down.

Faith smiled. "See, he won't hurt you."

Kirby leaned down to get a better look. "He is beautiful."

Blake licked her face and she laughed. There was a vicious growl from behind her, which made Blake take a step back from her.

Kirby noticed that Faith frowned and shook her head and then looked at Kirby. "You ready to go inside now? Because my brother Bengie can only entertain Remy and Sara for so long."

Kirby nodded. "Yes, I'm fine now. Can Blake come inside? He'll keep me calm."

A wicked smile spread across Faith's face. "Don't worry, Kirby. Blake would love to play doggy, wouldn't you, Blake?"

Kirby kept her fingers in Blake's fur as they walked toward the house. Blake whined slightly, but followed her. The growling behind her continued, and curiosity got the better of her and she looked over her shoulder to see where it was coming from. The first man's lips were pulled back and canine-like teeth were showing.

Kirby turned back to Faith. "You sure it's okay for me to stay this weekend? Because he doesn't look or sound very happy about it."

Faith waved him away. "Don't worry about Rane. He's always got a stick up his butt. Actually, he's going to go get your stuff out of your car. Aren't you, Rane?"

Rane looked at Kirby intently for a moment. His electric blue eyes sparkled and his growling stopped, then his mouth formed into a grin as he nodded, holding out his hand.

She dropped the keys in his hand, careful not to touch him, but before she could move away he grabbed her hand and held it, just looking at her. Eventually he brought her hand to his mouth and kissed it, his eyes never leaving hers. He sighed, dropped her hand, and turned, walking away.

"Holy shit," Faith said as they turned and entered the large house overlooking the water.

* * * *

Rane couldn't believe it. He'd found his mate, and it was Kirby. As soon as he'd opened the door, the smell hit and almost brought him to his knees. She smelled of apple and cinnamon, his favorite.

She was magnificent. When he saw her face, he fell instantly in lust. She had fire engine red hair, curling just past her shoulders, and big brown eyes with a light dusting of freckles on her pert little nose. When she got out of the car, his dick instantly got hard. Kirby was short, about the same size or maybe even a little smaller than Faith's five feet three. She had full, plump breasts, definitely bigger than any woman he knew. He loved that she was fuller around the waist, just the way he liked it. He always thought Faith and his sisters were too skinny, he liked women with some meat on their bones.

Kirby wore shorts to her knees and a t-shirt that revealed a bit too much breast for his liking. Her voice was like music to him. Rane fought his wolf the whole time, especially when she touched Blake. Thank God for Kane holding him back, as he had almost cracked, changing into wolf form.

As he grabbed the two small suitcases from the car, he smiled at the thought that she'd be there all weekend. Rane knew he must look like a fool, because he couldn't keep the huge smile off his face as he walked into the house.

Chapter 2

Kirby felt great...fantastic. For once in her life she wasn't the oddball, the weird kid that loved animals and had too many of them. Her mother had always said that all the Burns girls loved animals and she was just more sensitive. Even her father's family, the Browns, were sensitive to animals. Kirby had moved a two-and-a-half-hour drive away from her parents and brothers, to start anew. She wanted to make some friends her own age, or as her brothers said, the same species. Now that she had accomplished the friends part she was going to try dating a guy without one of her brothers scaring him away. She laughed. If her brothers could see her now...

"What's funny?" asked Remy as they came in from outside.

"Ha! My brothers always said I was boring and too shy to do anything but sit at home with all of my animals. I don't know if they would believe everything I've done since meeting you all." They all laughed. Kirby smiled as she added, "Don't worry, I'm going to send them pictures on my phone, that will shut them up." *Or*, she thought, *send them here to check on me.* Feeling more relaxed now, she let go of Blake's fur.

"So, I see you've met one of Faith's dogs," said Remy as Blake wandered off. "I haven't seen this one before. He's beautiful." A huge grin came over Remy's face. "The one Faith seems to like the most is this huge, horse looking wolf with dirty blond colored hair and bright blue eyes. Argh." Remy shivered. "Gives me the heebie-jeebies every time I see him. Now that I think about it, he kind of reminds me of Kane. That's probably why I react to him like that, because they're both big arse nasty dogs."

Faith shot a glare at Remy, and they seemed to have a silent talk for a moment before Faith looked at Kane. Then Remy doubled over laughing. Kirby looked up behind Faith to see Kane giving Remy a deadly stare.

"Oh, be nice, Remy, it's my birthday. How about we decide which bands are priority to see?"

Faith grabbed Kirby and Remy's hands as they walked into a large lounge room with a huge plasma hanging on the wall, surround sound stereo system, PlayStation, Xbox, Wii, and heaps of games—you name it, it was there. The room was any male's paradise.

"Wow," Kirby mumbled. She took a seat in the middle of the sofa with Faith and Sara on either side, discussing when they would leave and what bands were priorities.

Kirby couldn't keep the smile off her face. She had never had this before...friends that she could laugh and argue with, and now Faith even knew her secret ability. She finally felt like she belonged.

* * * *

Rane came into the house to laughing, screaming, and squealing. He waited in the entry hall, watching and listening.

"Oh my God, they didn't. What did you two do?"

He heard the musical voice of Kirby answer, "Well, Faith must be used to it because she handled it like a pro. I tell you what though, damn! That is not what fifteen to sixteen year olds look like where I'm from. If they did, I wouldn't still be a virgin at twenty-two years old." All four girls squealed with laughter.

Rane would swear his wolf did a happy dance that she was untouched and only they would have her.

Sara giggled. "Faith, you have to tell, give it up."

"Okay, but I laughed my arse off when it happened. I don't know if I can tell it. You know how I told you that after school care is in the converted gym? Well, it was myself and Kirby's turn to set up, which involves a lot of moving around and lifting. I noticed we had a crowd of boys about the age of fifteen-sixteen. They were finishing up playing basketball. The coach usually always tries to stay back if he knows Kirby is going to be there."

Kirby chimed in, "He does not."

Rane bit his tongue so he wouldn't growl. He didn't want them to notice him and stop talking. Rane stepped toward the doorway and peeked into the lounge room, watching as they threw food at each other.

"Hey, don't waste the M&Ms," Remy said, which for some reason made them fall to the floor in giggling fits.

"Don't listen to Kirby, he does stay back for her, and if the PE teachers or coaches at the school I went to looked like him, I would probably be a soccer or basketball star," commented Faith. All the girls squealed in laughter.

Kane came up beside Rane with his work bag in hand. "I know I've retired from the military, but someone has to keep an eye on things, so while you're gone, I'll check on your recruits. Do you still think you can do this? I know what she is to you."

"Hell yes, I'm going. I'm not an idiot. I am not going to run from my mate. I'm going to embrace this with open arms. You're running right now, aren't you, Kane?"

"God yes! You do hear them, don't you? I love that woman in there, but when she's with those friends..." He shivered. "Good luck with them today. Watch those women like a hawk."

Kane left and deliberately slammed the door. Faith turned toward it and said, "Oh, there's Rane. Let's go. I don't want to get there too late."

He smiled and nodded at them, then turned around and headed out the door, knowing that they were following him.

* * * *

By late afternoon, Rane had figured out that he was in hell. A straight guy never goes out with women on a girls' day out, no matter what they're doing or where they're going. He should have taken Kane up on the offer to bail out. It was worse still, because if one more person accidently touched Kirby's butt, boobs, waist, or any other body part, he was going to rip them apart. Not to mention the men who asked for her number...they were going to die. The worst thing of all was that she ignored him, wouldn't even look at him, avoided being close to him. By the time night fell, his wolf was so on edge that he did something he never did, he retreated and called Kane.

"Okay, who do I have to get to replace me? I can't watch without touching her or breaking some bones in these guys that she's attracting."

Kane chuckled. "Not to worry. I'm coming, I'll be there in a couple of minutes, and then we can endure together."

He shut his phone as Jamie, Devlin, Owen, Cullen, Dominic, and Tray came up next to him. "We heard the good news, bro. Good luck with that one, she is hot."

Rane whacked Jamie upside the head. "Does anything but shit come from your mouth?" He turned to Tray. "How the fuck did Kane get you to do this, Tray?"

Tray frowned. "He didn't, I'm in the same boat as you."

Rane raised his eyebrow.

"Sara," Tray explained.

Rane laughed. "When?"

"Kane's thirty-fifth birthday party, but she was still seeing that dick then. They broke up a week and a half ago, so I've been biding my time. I knew she'd be staying with Faith this weekend. Don't worry, Rane, I know how you feel. The guys have been holding me back. That last guy that came up to her nearly didn't leave here alive."

Rane nodded, glancing over at Faith only to notice that she had gone still. Fuck, she was going into one of her trance visions. She was pushed from behind and started falling. All seven werewolves ran straight to Faith, but Remy, Sara, and Kirby caught her right before she hit the ground.

Rane's Mate / Hazel Gower

Rane picked Faith up, and even he could feel that this was going to be a big vision. He yelled over the noise to call Kane and see how close he was. The six werewolves surrounded the women, protecting them from any danger or prying eyes.

Rane was surprised when Sara spoke up. "This is not the place for her to be having one of these." All the wolves turned to stare at her. Sara rolled her eyes. "She's been one of my best friends for sixteen years. My God, I'm a water element myself. I know you guys are something paranormal, but she would never tell us what."

All the werewolves turned to Remy and waited for her to tell what element she was. Groaning, she reluctantly told them. "Okay, fine, I'm a fire element. You can all stop looking at us now. You expected Faith to keep your secret, so she also kept ours."

Faith was snatched out of Rane's arms and the wolves stood to attention as Kane took over. "How long has she been out? Who was around? Did she touch anyone?"

"Five minutes tops," Rane said. "I didn't notice anything suspicious, and no, she wasn't touching anyone." He turned to the women. "Did any of you see her touch anyone? Did you notice anything suspicious?"

Kirby moved forward, speaking up. "No. I only felt

you seven wolves, though there is a cat shifter somewhere out there, but I don't know if it's male or female."

Remy and Sara looked at her in surprise. "You're a what?" Sara asked.

Kane interrupted, "Not here. Not now. We need a safe place."

Taking out his phone, Kane made a call and five minutes later they were all backstage in a medical tent. Once everyone else was cleared out, the twelve of them sat quietly, too scared to say anything. They all waited for Faith to come out of her vision. Kane held her tight on his lap.

Faith came out of the vision, panic stricken. "You need to call more wolves." She rubbed her forehead. "Honey, massage my head, I saw too much in such a short period of time. Fuck, Remy, Sara, and Kirby...where are they?" The three women came into her line of vision. "I'm sorry, but I'm going to say a lot of weird stuff and I'll have to explain it later." She turned to the werewolves. "I'm so sorry if I say something I shouldn't." Everyone nodded. "Here it goes—psychics, elements, and sensors must be drawn to each other. We must all love music because there are a lot of us here today. So what do you think is going to happen tonight? Demons, minions, and zombies are coming."

Kirby and Sara laughed. "Um, very funny. They're all

make believe," Sara commented.

Faith smiled sadly at Sara and Kirby. "I'm so sorry to drag you into this, but they are real. The military knows all about them, and they make sure it stays hush-hush." Faith turned back to the werewolves. "Tonight is going to be major. The demons are working together in large groups, they're desperate for these people."

She turned and focused on Rane. "You're going to have to get military help, as I don't know how we're going to contain this. I saw four groups of people the demons want." She pushed off Kane and started to pace. "In the first group I saw two women. They are both some kind of element. I think they're in their late twenties-early thirties. They were both blondes, one with blue eyes, the other green. They both had jeans on. One had a black lace top, the other had brown sequins, and they were coming out of the techno beat shed. One of the side doors was near gates and I saw three demons, and I did a quick count and I think there were eight minions and two zombies. That was all I got because it flashed to the next one really quickly. The only definite I got was the demons.

"The second group is the one we need to focus on as they want them bad. I've never seen this many demons work together. Eight demons." Faith shook her head. "They want the people… They're just teenagers. There are five of them, all are something paranormal. I only got a definite of two though, the important ones. One boy is like me and the other boy is similar to Kirby. Minions were everywhere, I couldn't get a sure count, there were four zombies maybe."

Faith started shaking. Kane stopped her pacing and hugged her close, assuring her that his father was listening and he had Major Black listening on another phone.

She settled into Kane's hold and continued on. "They're near the small stage. This group is in a band, and they played earlier this morning and stayed to watch the other bands. This is the youngest of the four groups the demons want, and they're all males. I feel this one is going to go down around about ten-thirty or eleven PM. They're going to leave via the left side exit off the backstage, all the boys together. It was too quick, and that's all I got. The only thing I can remember about them is that one had a mohawk and the other had lots of piercings on his face. Sorry," Faith apologized again. "Too much was going on."

Faith continued on as Rane looked around the room, noticing the intent stare of all the wolves and the women. He returned his attention to the conversation as the werewolves swore, and then the room turned quiet. His brother told their dad that they were going to need every available wolf there now.

Hanging up the phone, Kane looked at Rane. "Please tell me that you have trained the six human military men enough, because we're going to need all the help we can get."

Rane sighed, running his fingers through his hair. "They will have to do. If we split them up, put two in each team, they should be fine." He got on the phone, making sure everything was organized.

Kane swore, pounding his fist, before he turned back to him. "Rane, the weapons aren't all iced."

Sara cleared her throat. "I'm a water element, what do you mean by iced?"

Rane smiled at Kane, pulling one of his blades out as he explained to Sara how everything worked. Sara was confident she could ice the tips.

Faith interrupted them, speaking loudly so the whole room could hear, which now consisted of all of the werewolves they could spare, six military men, and three women.

"We need to try to make this look like part of the show. We want the least amount of pandemonium. Sara, Remy, and Kirby have agreed to help. I know already that Sara and Remy work well together. I'd like for them to be put with—

"

Tray stepped forward. "If you're putting Sara in danger, she goes with me."

Sara stared at Tray bug-eyed and open-mouthed.

Kane spoke up. "Tray, you're my best marksman shooter with bow and arrows. I need you elsewhere."

"I mean you no disrespect, but my mate stays with me."

Kane nodded and Faith smiled.

Sara sputtered out, "Mate…I am not…"

Tray went straight over to Sara and looked into her eyes and said, "Yes, you are." He pulled her shirt to the side and bit her shoulder.

Sara screamed, and then moaned. Several chuckles were heard when she pushed on his head, smacking it. "You arsehole, you bit me."

Rane chuckled as they continued to bicker. Faith and Kane gave more instructions.

Finally Faith looked at Rane and said, "Kirby and I are going with you in the second group." Faith advanced on him, her finger pointed at his chest. "Don't you do anything like Tray just did. I'm going to kick his arse later if Sara allows him to live. I mean it, Rane."

He put his hands up. "I will not bite her tonight."

"Okay, let's go and get into position, and remember, minimal damage."

Pulling out into their groups, Rane looked at his group which consisted of Kane, Jamie, Devlin, Blake, Major Samuel Black, Sergeant Nathan Cross, and Dominic, Seth, and Owen in wolf form, also Faith and Kirby.

Chapter 3

Kirby was trying not to freak out. A few hours ago she had found out that her new friends were supernaturals and that other beings existed, like werewolves, demons, and other terrifying things. Oh, and that demons wanted to take over the world, kill almost all of humanity, and any humans that were left made to be their slaves or zombies. The thing that had her scared shitless though was that in a crazy moment she had agreed to help.

They got themselves in as much of a position as possible. Kirby couldn't understand how the demons were going to do this when they were surrounded by people. "How on earth do they expect to pull this off? There are people everywhere."

"They think the chaos they'll cause will help them get the people they want. And sad to say, but it most definitely will. As everyone will be trying to get away, they'll be going in the opposite direction." Faith glanced at all the people near the stage then turned back to her. "Let's hope the demons come when the last band has finished, then almost everyone will have moved to the main stage."

Kirby looked around to see the band was finishing their

last song. Biting her lip, she turned to Faith. "How long do you think we have? The band is finishing now and we all seem to be spread pretty thin."

Faith didn't get to reply as Rane came strolling over and cut her answer off. "Tell me you gave Kirby a weapon so she's not just standing around looking like a stunned mullet."

Kirby ignored Rane's comment. She didn't even bother to acknowledge him. Every time she thought about him or even glanced his way her stomach did weird little flips.

She smiled when Faith rolled her eyes before turning to him. "Of course, although I don't know what good they will do her. She has had no training. First thing tomorrow I'm going to teach the girls some basic moves." Faith reached forward and patted his arm. "Try not to worry. I'll protect her."

Rane groaned. "Oh God, now I feel real great. Why didn't we just send the girls home? Dad, Mum, Bengie, and the girls would have looked after them."

Kirby felt her stomach sink. Fantastic, Rane didn't even want her around.

Faith sighed. "We couldn't spare anyone to drive her home, and I kind of wanted to try a little experiment with Kirby."

Kirby turned to Faith. "What experiment?"

"I was hoping you would help with the minions as they are kinda animals."

"No fucking way, Faith. I know what you're thinking. Kane, control your mate," Rane muttered.

"Idiot," Faith and Kirby huffed out.

Faith and Kirby shook their heads as Faith glared at Rane. "You did not just tell Kane to control me. If we didn't have demons coming right now I would so be kicking your arse."

"Faith, I want to help, tell me about this experiment."

"You said you can talk to animals, so maybe you can get minions to do what you want, or at least confuse them enough for me to kill them."

Kirby touched her forehead, feeling a migraine coming on. "Well, if I can see the eyes of an animal—"

"I said no. You are not looking a minion in the eye, no frigging way." Rane glared at her.

Fuck this idiot. What right did he have to tell her what to do? She'd moved away from her overbearing, controlling brothers so she didn't have to put up with stuff like this. She'd had enough. Rane might be the best looking man she'd ever laid eyes on, but he was a controlling arsehole just like her brothers. She turned to Rane, her fists clenched at her sides.

"You do not get to tell me what to do. You've been glaring at me all day long and made it perfectly clear to everyone that you do not want me here. I don't care if you're the hottest guy I've ever seen, you are a controlling arsehole. I pity the woman who gets stuck with you."

Kirby heard laughter behind her, which turned to covered coughs as Rane turned and growled at his brothers. "Well, guess what, little red? That woman is—"

Faith interrupted them. "Not now, Rane. It's showtime."

Kirby turned from Rane to see they were surrounded. She screamed, even knowing she shouldn't as it would draw attention to her. But at the sight of the minions, she couldn't help it.

"Kirby, get it together," yelled Faith.

It took her a minute to gather herself. There were screams everywhere. Faith was right, most people had moved to the big stage, but the few that were still around were screaming and trying to get away so they wouldn't be slaughtered.

Kirby saw creatures that were a mixture of a small, fat pig, but gray and black instead of pink, and a bat, but the wings had sharp thorns all over them. The little creatures also had sharp teeth.

Faith yelled over to her, "If you can't control them, then you'll have to kill them. The best way is to cut the wings off first and either chop off their heads or stab their heart, but give it a try to control them before you attempt the other."

Sighing, Kirby looked up, nodded at Faith, then turned to look at the minions. She stilled though when she saw a demon. Frozen, staring at the things out of nightmares, Kirby looked at eight huge beasts ranging in size from ten to sixteen feet. They were built like a tank and were bright red with black thorns all over their exposed skin. Two large, black horns protruded from their head. They had wicked, long teeth, and had a tail with an arrow spike on the end. Some had two arrow spikes on their tail.

Kirby almost fell over when Faith elbowed her, which helped her get out of her frozen, terrified stare. "Focus, Kirby. We don't have time for you to be scared now. You need to give your powers a try. But whatever happens, stay away from the demons and don't look into their eyes. Pull out the knife I gave you just in case." Faith pulled out two long knives, almost like machetes. "Go, Kirby. I need you to guard the backstage door so they don't get these kids." Faith ran to the stage door with her and placed one of the huge machete knives across the doors, jamming them shut.

Faith turned to Kirby. "Get ready, because here they come."

Kirby glanced up to see twelve minions coming at her and Faith. Looking at as many as she could, she sought their thought pattern and came up against violence, death, and pain. She strained to push further into their minds, searching for any commands. Eventually she found the command she was looking for. They had been ordered to *Hurt, kill as many as you can, but don't kill this group–just corner them.* A picture flashed in her mind of a group of teenage boys. This command repeated over and over in the minions' minds. Focusing as much as possible, Kirby changed the command just as she felt the minions starting to bite her legs and their wings cutting into her face.

She could hear Faith yelling, "Now, do it now."

Screaming in the minions' head, she said. "Freeze, stop, freeze."

Ten minions froze in their spot, turning their ugly heads from side to side with a look of confusion.

Kirby turned to Faith, yelling over the screaming. "Hurry I don't know long I'll be able to hold them off."

"Brilliant!" Faith yelled.

As Faith continued to run and almost dance about, chopping and cutting wings and heads off the minions, she yelled over her shoulder, "Guard the stage doors, Kirby. Zombies are coming. Don't be fooled by their human appearance. Kill them if you can."

Kirby's back hit the stage door as a hand reached out and grabbed her hair. Screaming and kicking, she tried to get out of the hold. She heard Faith yelling at her again to use her knife and kill. Pulling her knife around, Kirby slashed at the hand holding her hair and turned to see something that was once human. Shutting her eyes, she stabbed its chest.

Turning to find Faith finishing up on three zombie creatures, she said, "Wow, you're a modern day Buffy."

Faith smiled then screamed in pain as a sixteen foot, hulking demon grabbed her from behind. Kirby stared, transfixed, never having seen anything like it. Faith used her knifed hands above her head, slicing backward. She spun, moving her hands down, then pushed both her knives up and into the demon's chest. The demon's scream was deafening.

Faith never seemed to stop as she yelled to Kane, "Get your arse over here now."

The demon was trying to pull the knife out with one hand and reach for Faith with his other hand, his tail snaking toward her. Afraid to blink because she might miss something, Kirby watched as Faith quickly maneuvered out of the way. Kane ran over, jumped on the demon's back, climbing to his head, which he then cut off. Staring opened-mouthed, Kirby looked at the chaos around her. Eight dead demons, four zombies, and about forty minions lay scattered on the ground. Injured people were lying everywhere.

Faith and Kane came over to her, smiling. "Kirby was amazing, Kane. I really think we could help train her on a larger scale to freeze the minions, or command them to do other things. Even with no practice and never doing anything like this before, she got them to freeze for a couple of minutes, which gave me time to kill them. I feel, no, I *know* she could do it for a lot longer."

Kane smiled at her, nodding as he said, "You did real good, Kirby. Thanks for the help. I now need to know how badly you were hurt?"

"I'm fine," she assured Kane. "Look after Faith first."

Kane ran his fingers through his hair, sighing. He looked his mate up and down. "Faith has hardly got a scratch on her, and the scratches she does have will be healed in five to ten minutes tops. Trust me, if she was hurt I would tend to her before I did anything else." He leaned down and brushed his lips against Faith's, whispering, "I love you, princess."

Kirby grinned as she glanced at Faith. "Yeah, she is super-fast."

Faith laughed. "I was Kane's shadow when I was little. I went to all their fighting lessons until they finally caved and taught me to fight properly."

Kane leaned down again and kissed Faith's forehead. "The army has called in reinforcements to help clean up. I thought since I'm a doctor I would help out too, but only if that's okay, princess?" Faith nodded her head. "I only stayed over here because Rane would kill me if I didn't check Kirby out first."

Shaking her head, Kirby moaned. "He is so overbearing. I really pity the poor woman—" Kane's chuckle cut her off. Kirby sighed. "I really am fine, Kane, just some cuts and scratches. I don't think it's anything serious."

Kane walked closer to her. "Let me just have a quick look." Carefully, he checked her over, stopping at the deep cut on her arm. "I don't like the look of a couple of bites and cuts, but this cut on your arm will definitely need some stitches."

She winced when Kane gently touched the deep cut on her arm. She took a couple of steps back as she heard a loud growl. "What the fuck are you doing to her, Kane? I thought with you being my brother and a doctor that you would be gentle."

Kane rolled his eyes, then winked at her. "I just touched her arm. She's fine, Rane, but she is going to need stitches. Since she's a childcare worker, I know she's up to date with all of her shots. She did really well to come out of her first minion fight with only some bites and one major cut."

Rane looked at her, his electric blue eyes caught hers and she straighten her back and stood to her full height of five-four...well three and a half, but she rounded it up.

She glared back at him. "What does it matter to you? See, I survived, and Faith's experiment worked. So stick that where the sun doesn't shine." Before she lost her nerve she turned her back on him and walked over to Faith, who she didn't realize had left and was now talking to the group of teenagers.

* * * *

Rane smiled, his little red was as fiery as her hair. Kane chuckled and patted him on the back. "Good luck with that one. You're definitely not her favorite person."

"She'll get over it."

Kane laughed. "This is going to be so much fun to watch."

"Your relationship turned out in the end."

Kane laughed harder. "I really do feel sorry for her."

Rane ground his teeth. "The major is looking for you. Aren't you supposed to help with the medical?"

Kane nodded, still laughing. "Yes, but some overbearing werewolf wanted me to check their mate first. Also, I'm not the only one Major Black wanted to see."

"Great, fine, thanks, I'll see you back at your house. I know it's going to be a late night." He grinned at Kane. "Good luck to you. After everyone leaves, the girls are going to want to discuss it and get more information. You probably won't get any rest at all tonight." Rane walked away chuckling.

Kane yelled out, "Coward."

Rane found Major Black and several other army personnel setting up work stations.

Major Black turned to him. "I have contained everything, no one can get out or in. The security is working with us, and we have the media contained, telling them it was a terrorist attack. We were lucky that only a minimal amount were killed. Most are injured. It's amazing more weren't killed. I just had confirmation that the last group of demons have been killed at the main stage. The reinforcements are ready, at all exits and weak points."

Rane nodded. "Can we start letting some of the civilians out of the containment zone? Let's get rid of those people who don't know what happened. I'd like for as few people as possible to know what really went on tonight. So anyone who was attacked, or knows that it wasn't a terrorist attack, or was part of the show, keep them here for debriefing."

The major nodded. "We feel this is a major statement of things to come. We're stepping up our program and sending you six more of our top men. They'll be arriving within the next two days. A national meeting will be held in three days."

Rane raked his hand through his hair and grinded his teeth in frustration. "I expected as much. I agree, this was a huge statement. We need to organize a backup plan for any other major events."

The major nodded and moved in closer and said, "I would also like Faith and the alpha to attend the meeting."

"I'll talk to them about it."

"We have problems that cannot be discussed here, Rane. I'll come by the base tomorrow at nine hundred hours. See you then." The major turned away, gathering one of his teams.

Rane turned and gathered up his human military team.

They all looked in pretty bad shape. Sighing, he looked every one of them in the eye before he told them the new information. "Command is sending six more of you sorry lot tomorrow. I need you all back at base now. Get some sleep. You all look like shit. Tomorrow is going to be a big day. You will join a night patrol."

Rane looked down at his watch. 1:45 flashed. He let out a long, draw-out groan. He needed to go talk to Kane and his brothers about the new military news he'd just been told. With Arden away for another two months he had to find someone else to help him with all of these extra humans. Not to mention in the mess he had made with his mate. He needed to woo and claim her.

Chapter 4

Kirby looked around at Faith's packed house. All the new werewolves she had met, plus some she hadn't yet, were filling the huge house.

Glancing around again, she told herself she wasn't looking for him, but when she spotted him in the corner talking to a werewolf that she hadn't seen before, Kirby fought herself not to sigh. Looking Rane over from his massive feet, and slowly moving up his toned, leather-clad legs to his muscle-clad, tight white shirt, Kirby involuntarily licked her lips and bit her tongue to stop herself from sighing. Damn! She couldn't help it, Rane's body was what she imagined a god would look like. She glanced up at his face, sighing, he was better than a god. When she noticed his full lips turned up in a smirk, her head shot up to his eyes only to groan when she saw him staring straight at her. Shit, shit, shit, she'd been caught. Staring into Rane's eyes, she didn't dare turn away, especially when the bastard's smirk turned into a full-blown smile.

Groaning, she turned her head away, hoping to find someone she knew. Kirby saw Sara looking around frantically for someone to save her as Tray was coming her way.

＊ ＊ ＊ ＊

Coming over, Rane patted Tray on the shoulder as he noticed Tray's mate had walked away after yelling at him.

"Well, at least your mate is talking to you and knows she is your mate. Mine has no clue."

"Yeah, she said that she thinks I'm hot and I caught her checking me out earlier, but then she went on about how we're not mated or whatever the hell we werewolves call it. Then she said something about me not having meet her family, or even gone on a date. Argh, women are so confusing!"

Rane chuckled. "I agree one hundred percent."

Faith came up on her tiptoes to whack both of them on the back of their heads. "You are both idiots." She whacked them on the head again. "What have you two done to my friends? You werewolves have no clue about women. You are so lucky it's my birthday weekend and they can't run away, because I'm telling you now, I'm the only reason those girls are still here. I heard some of that conversation and I will spell it out for you, Tray, like I would one of my six-year-olds."

She turned to Rane. "You might want to listen too." Turning back to Tray, she continued. "Sara has been planning her wedding since she was a little girl. For Christ's sake she has a book with picture cutouts of dresses and cakes. She also loves her family and is a major daddy's girl, through and through, so if I were you, I would woo her and give her a big wedding, meet her parents, and give me a chance to wear one of those ugly bridesmaid dresses. Suck it up, not all women are like me. Go home, tomorrow come with some peach roses—they're her favorite. If I find out that you have humiliated her again, you'll wish that you were dead. Got it? Do I need to say that slower?"

Tray stared wide-eyed at Faith and nodded his head as he replied. "Got it, woo her, family, big wedding, all of that crap." He growled as Faith kicked him and shooed him away to a room full of werewolves' laughter.

Chuckling at his sister-in-law shooing away one of the meanest enforcers, Rane was too distracted to see Faith elbow him in the stomach.

"I would so not be laughing, Rane. Your mate thinks you're an arsehole and that you don't like her."

"What! Why would she think that?"

Faith shook her head, muttering. "Dumb idiots, all of them. Look, the way you acted tonight made it look like you didn't want her there, or fighting with us. I, and all the werewolves, know why you acted the way you did, but she's human, so she doesn't. Think about it, what do you think she thinks? I'll give you a hint, she definitely doesn't think she's your mate. She's not too fond of you. She just got away from her controlling brothers."

"Fuck! What am I supposed to do? You said not to claim her tonight."

"Idiot." She yelled the next bit, looking at every werewolf in the room. "If I find out that anyone claims their mate like Tray did with Sara, I will personally castrate them. A girl wants to get to know a man first, or at least meet him more than once before she's mated for life." She turned away from the group and back to him. "Talk to her, Rane, get to know her. Stop with the frigging insults, be nice. Do you know what that means? Give a compliment."

"I have had a relationship with a woman, Faith."

Faith punched him.

"Ouch! What was that for?" he asked, rubbing his chest. She might be little but she was lethal.

"I hit you because you're a fucking idiot. Your mate is not just some woman, this is the one woman meant for you." She turned and walked away, headed in the same direction that Kirby and Sara went.

Kane walked up, patting him on the back. "What did my evil mate do to you to give you that look?"

Rane turned to Kane. "Are you sure that your mate is only twenty-one tomorrow? Because sometimes I swear she's older."

Kane smiled. "I know, it is freaky. Sometimes I even forget." They sighed, both shaking their heads.

"What did the elders and Dad say about tonight?" Rane asked.

"Everyone is worried more than ever. This was bold of them, the demons did this in full view of the public, not just back alleys and small places. This was a major statement." Kane raked his fingers through his hair as he continued on. "I'm really worried about Faith. She's having a lot of visions, and she even talks in her sleep sometimes. She said something the other night that terrified me—all mates will be found to intervene and help with the balance, many will come from places that they shouldn't have been. If they are not found, demons will rule this world."

"Holy shit."

Kane shook his head. "I don't know how far and wide Faith wants us to look for people's mates. I don't even know if she's just talking about our pack, or the whole world's werewolves and weres population. I asked her when she woke up, but she told me it wasn't important for me to know at this time."

Rane felt sick. "This is huge. What have the other packs said?" He looked around, noticing every werewolf was quiet now, intent on their conversation.

"They're all fighting, wanting to send wolves over or for Faith to help, or for us to go over to their country or place and help find their mates and demon hidey-holes."

All the werewolves growled at this.

Kane continued. "We have found where Bengie was being held captive. We need to have your military teams ready by Thursday, because we're going underground to the demon fortress. Faith says that they're still there, but she doesn't think that they'll be there for long. I want Bengie to come, but Faith is not allowing it as she doesn't want him to live through that again. So, Rane, you need to have everyone ready by Thursday."

Rane gritted his teeth, knowing that they were going to be stretched to the limit.

Chapter 5

Kirby followed Sara outside where they found Remy sitting in an outdoor chair, literally playing with fire, throwing it from one hand to the other. Kirby and Sara pulled chairs out and sat on either side of her.

"They have a whole heap of us, you know. After they saved them from those things, they brought them back here," Remy said.

"Yeah, I think they're trying to sort something out with the people they saved tonight. Faith told me the same thing earlier."

Remy started crying. "Bengie won't come anywhere near me now. He says I probably hate him now that I know what he is." She cried harder. "It took me some time, but Faith finally explained that he is only a half-breed, that those creatures took Faith's biological mother and forced her to do unthinkable things with those demons. Faith says it's one of the reasons why they want us. They figure if we're strong enough to carry a werewolf child, we could carry one of theirs."

Kirby was shocked. "Every time I have meet Bengie he has been nothing but sweet. He's just like a little kid, and he doesn't have horns or thorns..." She trailed off.

"I know, but he is reddish and massive, he does have black eyes, and his skin is extremely hot." Remy sighed. "I know he has a crush on me. Right now I don't know myself. I don't know how I feel. That's why I'm out here. I need to think about everything. What about you two?"

Kirby thought over everything that had happened today. "They know now that we have paranormal gifts, so will they let us leave? Do you think that they will keep us?"

Sara and Remy frowned. "Who?"

"The werewolves." Kirby shook her head. "I want to help, don't get me wrong. I will admit that it felt good saving all of those people, but I'm nothing special for these werewolves to want to keep a hold of me."

Faith came up behind their chairs. "Yes, you are. We all are. We'll all play a part whether we want to or not." Faith pulled up a chair so she was facing the three of them. "Could you at least give my brother a chance? He's only twelve, believe it or not."

"Shit," Remy said.

Faith nodded. "He's innocent in all of this. I can only tell you what I know, and what I'm allowed to tell you, although you always have a choice."

"Why are you not allowed to tell us certain things?"

Kirby asked.

"I don't know why myself. Life is never easy, even when you're a regular human, but for those werewolves that are all around us, it's all they have ever known. They are told and taught from a young age that they are protectors of the earth."

Kirby butted in. "Why are you having a child and bringing it into all this? I love children, I work with them, but after seeing all this and helping you today I don't understand how you can bring a child into a world like that."

Faith smiled at her. "What does everyone need? Hope, everyone needs something to look forward to, something to fight for. I know good will always triumph over evil. We need a future. If all of us thought like you, we wouldn't have a future, and we all need to have hope and things to look forward to."

Kirby stared at Faith. "Are you sure you're only twenty-one? Sometimes the things you say..." She shook her head.

Faith laughed. "Yes. Unfortunately, when you see what I've seen you grow up fast." She seemed to go into a daze for a minute, shake herself, and continue on. "I will say this, all those werewolves here and around the world do what they do to make sure that everyone is safe. Just remember that they do deserve love, fun, friendship, and life. Give them a chance." She touched each of their hands, squeezing them gently. "Let's go to bed now. I know they have something huge planned for my birthday. Think about what I've said. You'll know by morning what you want to do. I know you will." Faith got up and walked back into the house.

Kirby turned to see Sara and Remy smiling. "Is she always like that? 'Cause it's nice to know that I'm not the only weird person out there." They hugged each other, laughing, which felt good and right. Then they walked back inside, following Faith into the now empty house.

* * * *

Kirby awoke in the afternoon to the sound of squealing. Climbing out of bed, she chucked a dress on, then went to the bathroom and did everything as quickly as possible. Then she followed the squealing only to crash into Sara and Remy.

"What the hell is going on?" Kirby asked.

"I don't know, I'm too scared to find out," said Remy.

They all laughed and walked into the lounge room together to see Faith making out with her husband.

"My God, are all werewolves' bodies the envy of the

gods?" Sara mumbled.

Remy groaned. "I didn't want to wake up to a nightmare."

Kane groaned as he pulled his lips from Faith. "Why, princess? Why is she your best friend? She is evil."

Faith laughed and turned to them. "Guess what Kane got me?"

Kirby smiled, she couldn't help it as Faith's mood was infectious, or so she thought until Remy said, "Ah, I don't know, did he knock you up so you can't drink today? No, can't be that 'cause he's already done that. Ah, I know...he mated you, after you only speaking to him a couple of times in four years? Nah, it couldn't be that either, because he's done that already too. How about he tries to push you away and you come to live with me again? That sounds good."

Kane groaned.

Faith chuckled. "Remy, you promised that this weekend you would be nice to Kane. Just because you know all the bad things doesn't mean that's all that he is."

Remy rolled her eyes. "Okay, okay, what did your mate—I'm sorry, but I'm not saying *husband* until he gives you a proper wedding—get you for your birthday?"

Faith's smile was huge. "Here's a hint, girls. Who is the one person in the whole universe that I would leave

Kane for?"

"*What!*" Kane said.

Faith patted Kane on the chest. "Honey, shush."

Kirby noticed that Remy's eyes had glazed over. "No, no way. How? No, that's impossible. I'll be nice to him forever. No, not forever, but he may get a month out of me."

Sara interrupted her, screaming, "Oh my God, Jeremy Sento."

Faith nodded, and Sara and Remy screamed.

"Who is Jeremy Sento?" Kirby asked.

All three girls screamed out, "Sixty Seconds to Venus."

Kirby knew that name—it was one of the hottest bands around—and she joined into the screaming and jumping.

* * * *

Rane came into the house to find Kane seated on the lounge and all four women squealing, screaming, and jumping up and down.

"What happened?" Rane asked.

"I told Faith about her present."

Tray came in with twelve peach-colored roses. "What part of the present?"

"I didn't even get past the Jeremy Sento."

The girls squealed again at the mention of this name.

"So she doesn't know the rest?" Rane asked.

"No." Kane frowned. "I'm not so sure it's a good idea now."

"What, why?" Tray said.

"Because apparently this Jeremy Sento is the man that she would leave me for."

Rane burst out laughing along with Tray. "No way," they both said.

"Ask," said Kane.

Tray smiled and turned to the women as he shouted over the squealing, "So this Jeremy whatever guy..." Tray glanced at Sara. "If by some miracle, he asked you to dump whomever you are with and be with him, would you do it?"

There was no hesitation at all as all four women laughed and as one said, "In a heartbeat."

Rane, Kane, and Tray growled, which just seemed to make the girls laugh and squeal harder.

Sara spoke up, "Come on, there has to be a woman you would forsake all others for, an ideal woman?"

"Yes," all three men said. "Our true mate."

The women groaned. "Are these guys for real?" Remy asked.

"Yes." Faith smiled. "Yes, they are. Don't you just love them?"

Remy made a fake vomiting sound as Faith made goo-goo eyes at Kane. Then her smile turned wicked. "But if Jeremy Sento wants me, I will say bye-bye." All the women laughed again.

Rane frowned, looking at Kirby. She had the same dreamy-eyed look as the other women. Turning back to Kane, he said, "I'm thinking we should cancel this before this Jeremy Sento leaves here in a body bag."

"Nooos" drowned out his last words.

Faith pouted at Kane. He sighed and shook his head. "Fine, this Jeremy Sento and his band will be coming tonight just for you and—"

Squeals drowned out the rest, and Faith threw herself at Kane. "I love you, I love you, I love you, I love you."

Kane and Rane chuckled. Kane hugged her tighter. "You need to thank my family for this one. Rane, Tray, who wants to tell her the rest?"

Rane smiled. "Just hold it for a minute, Mum and Dad are just about to come in the door."

Their parents came in, along with Griffen, Devlin, Jamie, Ava, Eve, Bengie, and his little sisters. Faith ran to her brother and hugged him. "Hey, buddy. I missed you." She pulled him the rest of the way into the group.

"Happy birthday, sis."

"I love you, Bengie."

He smiled, showing his sharp, shining teeth, and hugged her again.

Remy hesitantly came forward. "Hey, buddy, where is my hug? I'm so sorry for the way I acted."

Red tears ran down Bengie's face as he hugged Remy.

"Come on, big guy, I didn't mean to act the way I did." He nodded and hugged her tighter.

Faith's smile was huge and she said, "Let's go sit down, they're going to tell me what the rest of my birthday present is."

Eve and Ava couldn't seem to hold it in much longer. "It's a concert. We know from the squealing we heard that you know about Sixty Seconds to Venus. We also got some of your favorite local Australian bands."

The screaming and jumping continued again, with his sisters joining in. Jamie came over and patted Tray, Rane, and Kane's back.

"I thought you were smart, brother. Posters of him covered her wa—"

Whacking Jamie upside the head, Kane groaned out, "My God, shut up, Jamie."

Griffen stepped forward. "We'd just like to add how much we love and appreciate you," he told Faith. "This concert that we organized is to show all of that."

Crying, Faith hugged everyone in his family. "I love you all."

All the women surrounded her, hugging her again. The werewolves shook their heads, and Jamie spoke up. "Aren't you supposed to be happy?"

"I am, these are happy tears."

Rane looked at Kirby to find she was finally standing alone. Walking over to her, he gently grasped her arm and walked to the back door. "Can I have a word with you?"

Kirby glanced at him and looked back at Kane and Faith.

"I'm sure they want a moment or two. Please, little red."

She seemed shocked by his niceness and nodded her head as they continued out the door.

Once the door was shut he turned to her. "I'm sorry."

She looked at him like he had sprouted an extra head. "For what?"

He took a deep breath and looked into her big, brown eyes. "I'm sorry I don't know how to act around you. I didn't mean to offend you yesterday. I just didn't want you in danger."

She looked at him, studying his face. "Why? Why

would you care how you act around me?"

Grounding his teeth, he took another deep breath. This was harder than he thought it would be. "You're more than what I expected. You're beautiful, perfect even."

She stared at him open-mouthed. Snapping it shut, she said sarcastically, "Is this some type of joke?"

His brows furrowed. "No. Why would you think that?"

"Have you looked in the mirror lately?"

"What has that got to do with you being the most beautiful woman I've ever seen?"

She laughed at him so hard she held her stomach. "Now you're a joker—right?"

"No, I never joke."

"Okay." Kirby took several steps away from him. He pursued her until her back hit the wall of the house.

"Can I kiss you?"

Her eyes widened and she nodded slightly. He smiled, taking the last steps, and picked her up. She squealed as he dived in, taking her lush lips to his. He moved his hands to hold her up by her arse, and when she moaned into his mouth, he deepened the kiss and nipped her bottom lip. She gasped as his tongue snuck in. He then trailed kisses down her face and neck.

Kirby moaned and ran her fingers through his hair.

"Oh God, you're good. Oh yes."

Nipping at her shoulder, he groaned, knowing he had to pull away before he did something he shouldn't. He glanced up at her. She was so sexy right now. Her hair had fallen out of the messy bun she had it in, and it was now everywhere. Her eyes flashed with desire, and her lips were puffy and pink. God, he could stare at her all day long. The way she looked right now was about to make him come in his pants like a teenage boy.

"What's wrong?" she moaned.

He chuckled. "Not a thing. I just don't want to claim my mate against the back wall of Faith's house."

She instantly froze. "Your what?"

"My mate, you're my mate. I knew the moment I saw and smelled you."

"You're saying I smell!"

He chuckled again as, with a frown, she lifted her arms to check to see if she smelled. Then her frown turned into a glare. "Yeah—"

She whacked him on the chest.

"Ow! What did you hit me for?"

"I do not smell."

He released her and held his hands up in surrender as he rushed on. "Just let me finish. Yeah, you sure do. You smell like apple and cinnamon. It's my favorite."

She shook her head. "Are you sure? Maybe you got hit on the head last night by one of the demons. You're saying me, Kirby, me, I'm your mate?"

He chuckled. "Yep, I'm one hundred percent sure." He moved back, caging her against the wall again.

She pushed against his chest. "Do you not have a choice?"

Rane frowned. "I don't want a choice. I want you."

"But you're..." She moved her hand up and down and then pointed to herself and then pointed to him again.

"I don't get it."

She sighed. "You're gorgeous. What's wrong with you? Have all the other women had enough of you? Don't get me wrong, I'm not trying to be mean, but I just think you're a bit too good looking for me."

"What are you going on about, woman?"

"I'm just saying that you're way too hot for me. I mean, look at that body. I could maybe stretch myself to a five, but you're well over a ten, and fives and tens don't go together."

Rane stared at his mate. What was this woman going on about? "What do fives and tens have to do with anything? Let's forget numbers."

Kirby raised her eyebrow at him.

"I know I'm rough around the edges, but give me a chance. Get to know me."

"Well, I wouldn't call it rough, more like hard…very, very hard."

He shook his head, ignoring her last comment. "I took the military route in the family. I know I can be a bit controlling, like yesterday."

"Ha, controlling."

Grinding his teeth, he continued. "I would never hurt you. Come on, give me a chance to get to know you, and for you to get to know me. Be my date for the concert tonight. Please?"

"Err, I don't know. I'm here for Faith. I was here for Faith."

"I'll check with Faith, but I know she'll understand. If she's okay with it, then will you go with me?"

She nodded her head as they walked hand in hand back inside.

* * * *

A few hours later, Rane left Kane's house and headed to the human military base to meet the new recruits. He had also called a small meeting with Tray, Blake, Sebastian, and his brother Devlin. They needed to hear the news he had, and see the new recruits. He was hoping they would agree to help out.

He found them all waiting in his office. He told them what the military was going to do. "We need to brainstorm and talk about training strategies. I'm not looking forward to training fifty humans. I've already had huge problems convincing the six that are here that shooting the demons won't work. I was nasty enough to show them how wrong they were. We all know that demons absorb the lead, metal, it makes them stronger. I'm telling you, it took Arden and I a good twenty to twenty-five minutes to bring down the demon after having his powers boosted. I kid you not, they then suggested wooden bullets. Yeah, like that would work. It would just make them more pissed. I swear I've only just healed from that demonstration.

"We need to work out some things, since you lot are my best enforcers, and Arden and Tristan are in away teams for the next couple of months. I asked you to come today as I'll need help to put the new recruits down a peg or two. Show them the supernatural strength they're going to be working with. I've also been given the go ahead to expand outward. I've spoken to several of the world's alphas and they've spoken to their head human military. They've all decided that they need to take part and will be sending representatives from a couple of packs to see how we're working out."

He ran his fingers through his hair as he looked at all the wolves before him.

"America and England have only agreed to have one human military base, so we'll be getting extra recruits from England and America's packs, so we need to get ourselves ready. A lot have been given the choice to move and join our pack permanently. I'm in total agreement with this as it should make us stronger, although it will also make things harder as we'll have more work and many more recruits."

Rane looked around at his fellow werewolf friends. He knew what they were all thinking about. It was the same thing that clouded his mind at present. The enormity of what he had just told them and what it would mean for them.

Chapter 6

Getting ready for the dinner party and the big concert, Kirby smiled, because as usual all the women were running late. They had lost track of time this afternoon as they enjoyed the sun and sea at the beach, and they were now all nicely tanned, or burnt in her case. They were all in Faith's huge bathroom getting ready when she asked Faith for the second time, "Are you sure you don't mind Rane coming to take me? I feel so bad. I came to spend the weekend with you."

Faith laughed. "I'm fine. I'll have Remy, my brother, and Kane. After what I said this morning, my husband..." She glanced at Remy who raised her eyebrow. "...mate, is going to watch me like a hawk. You and Sara are meeting us there, and we'll all be sitting at the same table together. At the concert we'll definitely be together. Sorry, Remy, but I'm going to sneak back early and have some hot se—"

Sara's hands raised in surrender. "Okay, okay, we get it. We're to go out with these men and not feel guilty."

Faith laughed again and seemed to go into a trance for a minute or two, then looked at Sara. "Please, don't choose the red, because it's not my color, and think of poor Kirby, redheads and red do not go together. Oh, and say no to your dad, you are not waiting that long. I'm not going to be your bridesmaid six months pregnant. With a werewolf baby, that would mean I would be almost ready to pop."

All three women stared at Faith.

She stared back at them, raising her eyebrow. "What? I really don't like that red you have picked out."

Kirby giggled. "I hope I don't sound weird saying this, but Faith, I love you. You make me feel normal. It's so nice to have friends that are just as crazy as me." Kirby hugged Faith, Sara, and Remy.

Sara grinned. "Okay, I get it. No red bridesmaid dresses."

They were interrupted by Jamie. "If you guys just kiss, it would be just like my—"

Kirby, Remy, Sara, and Faith each picked up something and threw it at Jamie. He dodged everything, chuckling. "What?"

Faith laughed. "Jamie, you're a dick. Tell them we'll be out in five minutes and to never send you in again, or to allow you to volunteer."

"Argh, come on, Faith. Lately you're always taking the fun out of everything."

They all threw more stuff at Jamie and he grinned,

dodging them, then waved and walked away.

The laughter stopped as Faith turned to Sara and Kirby with a grin on her face. "I'll be sleeping in to really late tomorrow. Remy already volunteered to take Bengie bowling. I'll be sleeping in so late that you probably won't see me tomorrow. Maybe Monday morning before you leave for work I'll say bye."

Remy groaned. "This is so too much information."

Kirby bit her lip to stop from laughing.

"How come I get stuck going bowling, while you guys get to fuck those hot, hard-bodied men?" Remy asked.

Kirby stared at Remy, and Sara laughed; obviously comments like that were common from Remy. Walking out to the lounge room, they found Tray, Kane, Rane, and Bengie all dressed up and waiting for the four of them.

* * * *

Kirby arrived with Rane at a huge field area that was covered with tables galore, where groups of werewolves were sitting, relaxing and talking. She felt roughly a hundred wolves. They were easy to spot as all of them were freakishly tall and muscular. She would swear the smallest one was six-one and he was probably a teenager. You could even tell who the female werewolves were because they were stunning.

Kirby gulped and paused in her forward movement. She glanced at Rane and back to the werewolf women all around. Was he nuts?

Rane pulled her to a table. They sat close to Faith, and Kirby darted another glance around. A beautiful five-nine, gorgeous blonde came up and tried to sit next to Rane. He didn't even glance her way, he kept his eyes on Kirby as he introduced her to the woman. The woman smiled a sad smile and walked away.

Frowning, Kirby touched Rane's arm. "She could have sat next to you if you wanted. I could have sat with Faith."

His eyebrows furrowed as he frowned. "Why would I want to sit next to Sandra when I have you?"

He picked up her hand, which she'd placed on his arm, and kissed it, holding it against his lips. He smiled at the woman and man sitting across from them. Kirby was startled when she realized the couple was Rane's parents.

"I'd like you to meet my father Jack. He's the leader, as you would call him, but we call him the pack alpha."

Jack didn't look a day over forty. He had the same electric blue eyes and tanned skin as Rane. His hair was a dirty blond and he looked to be in the same good shape as all the werewolves.

She smiled. "Nice to meet you."

He nodded at her, then Rane pointed to the woman on Jack's right. "This is my mother Della."

This was Kirby's first real good look at the couple. She'd had a brief look at them that morning, but she would never have thought them to be his parents. His mother looked barely thirty-five years old. Kirby couldn't stop staring in amazement, and she couldn't turn away from their stares. Realizing she was being rude, she still couldn't disconnect from their stare.

When she noticed the table had gone quiet, she was embarrassed and finally turned her head away, apologizing. "I'm so sorry, I don't mean to stare."

The couple exchanged looks and smiled. Kirby frowned and looked around for help, as Rane didn't seem to be giving her any. Catching Faith's attention, Kirby saw her roll her eyes and take pity on her.

"You just looked into the eyes of two of the most powerful alphas in the world, and the only reason you eventually looked away was because of your human rules. You should feel good, you're one of only a small group who can look at these two alphas and not back down or turn away."

Rane looked at her and the smile on his face was huge. She was shocked as he leaned down and placed a quick kiss on her lips. She was curious now, so she asked, "Who else?"

"Remy can, but that is no surprise as she stands up to Kane, and he's also one of the strongest alphas and she speaks to him like no one else would dare. Kane is one of the biggest alphas in the world, that's why he was running the hospital emergency department at such a young age. When you take into consideration that he had been in the military for eight to ten years he's accomplished a lot to get to where he is in his career for his age."

Kane brushed his lips against Faith's head. "Thanks, princess." He rubbed Faith's shoulders. "You see, Kirby, every male in our family has done at least four years in the military, although our family is a rarity as all my parents produced were alphas. The military helps teach us control and discipline. I did eight years, and as you know Rane is still in."

Kirby glanced at Rane.

"Well, at the moment, I have my own kind of division of the military," Rane said. "Arden is still in the reserves, although he's joined my division now."

"Arden isn't here, about a quarter of us aren't as we have away teams," Kane explained. "Australia is a new country, so we only have six packs and they're stretched out to cover their territory. We cover New South Wales and Australian Capital Canberra, and another pack covers Queensland, another pack covers Western Australia, and so forth. As Australia is so young we are small, but as Australia grows older, we will grow. This all depends on how strong the alphas are, and who leads each pack."

The food was brought out and the men got up, telling the women to keep talking and they would fix them a plate.

Kirby nodded in acknowledgment at Rane as he left the table. Her brain right now was having an information overload. "Did I just pass some kind of test?"

Faith laughed. "Yes, but we would have still kept you even if you failed."

The men returned and Rane set a plate with a mountain of food on it in front of Kirby. Everyone went quiet as they ate.

Kirby smiled and ate everything on her plate without even realizing it as her mind was thinking about everything she'd just learnt.

Rane leaned over. "Do you want me to get you something else?"

Kirby groaned. She'd eaten too much already. "No, I'm fine, I couldn't eat any more."

Two hours later, the four girls stood in front of the

center stage as they laughed and giggled. The next act would be the one they'd all been waiting for.

"I think because I'm the birthday girl, I should get to get up on the stage with him." They all laughed as Kane growled.

Kirby glanced behind her to see three massive werewolves standing a stone's throw away with their arms crossed over their muscular chests.

Never having had this much fun in her life, she nudged Remy and giggled. "Maybe Remy could heat up the stage for us a bit. If it's hot, Jeremy might have to take off all of his clothes."

"I didn't know you had it in you, Kirby. That's the best idea you've had all night." Remy grinned, patting her on the back.

* * * *

Jamie came up behind them, chuckling. "Oh my God, you got your wife the worst birthday present. You are going to be killed by several werewolves tonight as their mates have gone crazy. I'm telling you guys, this Jeremy Sento has power over women."

Devlin, Griffen, and Blake joined in Jamie's laughter.

Jamie continued, "They haven't even noticed you guys since the concert started. Just imagine when this Jeremy

Sento comes onto the stage." Jamie was now doubled over laughing.

Rane smiled as Tray went over to his brother and whacked him hard on the shoulder, which almost caused Jamie to topple to the ground. "I so can't wait until you have a mate. Payback will be a bitch."

Rane whacked him on the back too. "You've got that right, Tray."

They walked over closer to their mates, finding them standing as close to the stage as possible. Tray looked at Kane. "How the hell did you get her favorite band to play?"

"I donated a truckload of money to their charities, and on top of that I offered them a ridiculous fee."

"Have you seen their video clips?" Tray asked. "I watched one earlier today, the one that's Sara and Faith's favorite, *Hurricane*, and after seeing that I can tell you now I would never have done what you did." He sighed, running his fingers through his hair. "Maybe I'm just old, but that film clip..."

"Don't worry, you're not old. I've seen it. It's filled with bondage and naked men and women, but that's how videos are these days," Rane commented.

Jamie and Devlin laughed. "You guys are so old. I have no idea how your mates are going to put up with you."

Tray, Kane, and Rane sighed in relief when Jamie shut up as his dad got onto the stage.

"Hello, everyone. I would like to say welcome and thanks for coming to this special night for Faith. This next act are our last guests of the night. While I have everyone together I would also like to welcome our new members, who are staying with us to help fight our cause, or just to stay and feel safe. We thank you all. But tonight was originally for one of our best girls, Faith. I personally don't know this band, but my daughters do and the birthday girl does. She's their number one fan, so, does she want to come up here and introduce them?"

Faith screamed at the top of her lungs. Kane seemed to reluctantly help her onto the stage. She kissed their father, grabbed the microphone, and turned to everyone.

"Thank you all for coming tonight and for my presents. I would also like to say that one of the reasons I love this band is because they support causes that better the earth. Without further ado, Sixty Seconds to Venus!"

Three men came out onto the stage and the women's screams became deafening. Rane chuckled as he noticed Kane holding his hand out to Faith to help her off the stage. Faith just stood there staring at, he assumed, Jeremy Sento. The man in question turned to Faith and said, "I understand that today is your birthday?"

All the werewolves chuckled as Faith stared wide-eyed and opened-mouthed. They had never seen her speechless.

Jeremy Sento looked around at all the werewolves, then his gaze fell on Faith's friends at the front, and Rane and several other wolves growled. Jeremy averted his eyes and gave an uncomfortable laugh.

"Luckily, we've been told what your favorite song is." He reached out and grabbed Faith's hand.

Rane and Tray grabbed Kane as he launched himself at Jeremy Sento. Faith leaned up to say something into Jeremy's ear. Kane did not like that at all, and Jamie came and helped them restrain him, grunting in frustration at having to hold a nine-five kg raging werewolf.

The lead singer smiled as he said, "Faith would like her three best friends to come up."

Rane and Tray let go and rushed to their mates, but they weren't quick enough. They were already on the stage. Faith kissed Jeremy's cheek, and Kane howled. Rane and about ten werewolves jumped on Kane. The bloody idiot still didn't fall to the floor.

Fifteen songs later, Rane was on the same page as Kane, and so was Tray. Having already figured out where to hide the body, Kane and Rane knew they could pull some strings so they wouldn't serve any time or be punished in any way. They were all in agreement to kill him, especially by the end of the last song when Kirby, Remy, and Sara went up on stage and kissed Jeremy on the cheek. The biggest problem was when Faith had to top her friends, so instead of the cheek, Faith took it too far and kissed Jeremy on the lips.

Jeremy ran for his life as Kane went after him, Faith trailing after them. The sound of a field of laughing wolves followed them.

Rane helped Kirby and Remy down from the stage. "I hope you don't plan to go back to that house, Remy, because I assure you when they catch each other, it will not be pretty, and the noises they are going to make will be heard for miles."

Remy and Bengie cringed.

"Argh! I'm so hoping I can block that image from my mind," Remy said. "Bengie, how about we go bowling, skating, to the movies, someplace where I can poke my eyes out?"

Bengie chuckled as Rane smiled at Remy. "I'll have three enforcers join you."

His sisters came up behind him. "We'll go too. Let's go have some fun."

Remy, Bengie, Ava, and Eve walked away.

* * * *

Kirby had never had so much fun in her life. Finally, she felt like she fit in. She turned to Rane as they walked along the beach. "I absolutely love your family. Your sisters are great, and Jamie and Devlin are so much fun. Tonight was the best night of my life."

He chuckled and paused and turned her to him. "It's not over yet."

Kirby flushed, and she reached up to cover her cheeks. She knew she must look as red as a tomato.

Rane grabbed her hands. "I like it."

Kirby mumbled, "I definitely made the right choice moving here."

They walked up the beach path and into the forest. "I'm going to show you my house, but it's not finished yet. I've been content to live in it as is, or at Arden's or Jamie's. You can change anything you want in it. The house, if you like it, will be yours, ours."

She stopped walking and stared at him. "What! Why would it be our house?"

He ran his fingers through his short hair and stared straight into her eyes. "You're my mate. Ever since I saw you I've been fighting my werewolf to keep from throwing you over my shoulder and taking you back to the house to mark you and claim you. It's been killing me not to touch you and hold you. The only reason I haven't let my wolf take over is because Faith said she would castrate me if I claimed you as my mate the same way Tray did with Sara."

Stunned, Kirby stared at him, delicious heat crawling up her body as the image of him throwing her over his shoulder and taking her to his house to claim her flashed in her mind. "Um, okay," she said before she realized what was coming out of her mouth.

Rane's eyes widened. "Um, okay to what?"

She really must have drunk too much or was deprived of something as a child, because she couldn't believe herself when she said, "Okay, you can mate me like that if you want."

Kirby didn't even seeing Rane move, but quick as lightning, he picked her up, throwing her over his shoulder, and ran through the last of the trees. The trees swam past her in a blur, and she got a quick glimpse at a one-story house with the second story half built. There was no pause as the door was opened and she glanced at a living room, then was rushed to a room with a massive bed and placed gently on it.

Rane took his shirt off and chucked it on the floor.

Kirby gulped. He was frigen huge, all muscular and toned. Backing up, she hit the headboard of the bed as Rane prowled toward her. His eyes were glowing an eerie blue, and his mouth was in a feral kind of smile. Shit! Maybe this was a bad idea. Maybe she was insane.

He growled. "These aren't your favorite clothes, are they?" She'd barely shaken her head when he continued, "I'll buy you new ones, of whatever you want."

His mouth captured hers, and with his tongue stuck in her mouth, she couldn't say anything, so she just nodded. He growled again, ripping the clothes from her body. Once she was naked, he seemed to take a breather and stare at her. Feeling hot all over due to embarrassment, she moved her hands to cover her body.

Through clenched teeth he ordered her, "Never cover yourself from me. You're perfect."

Kirby was terrified and thrilled at the same time. She slowly moved her hands away. Crawling on the bed, over her body, he kissed her mouth in the hottest searing kiss she had ever had. His hands moved leisurely down her body, exploring. She moaned into his mouth as his hand reached the special place between her legs. Slowly, gently, he probed and discovered places she never knew, giving her unimaginable pleasure. His mouth moved away from hers and down her body, kissing, sucking, and licking.

Never having experienced so much pleasure before, especially as his mouth joined his fingers, she cried out into a shattering orgasm. Rane licked and sucked the whole way through it and finally put one finger in her pussy, then he added a second. She could feel him gently stretching her as he sucked on her clit.

"Rane, Rraaannneee, I... I can't take any more. Please, please, please."

She didn't know exactly what she was begging for, but she knew there was more. Growling against her clit, he sent delicious tingles coursing through her body. "You taste even better than you smell. Come for me, my little red."

Adding a third finger in her pussy, he nipped her clit, and she came for the second time, moaning out his name. "*Rane!*"

Rane growled and leisurely moved back up her body, sucking, kissing, licking, and nipping here and there. She yanked his pants off and started to freak, because he was huge. Panicking a little and coming out of her sexual haze, she pointed at his penis.

"There's no way that will fit. You are way too big. I have never had one before this." That statement just seemed to make him hornier.

Smiling, he caught her mouth, murmuring against it. "Good, my little red. Good, good, only mine. We were made for each other. Don't worry, it will fit." He looked into her eyes. "I'll be as gentle as I can, but little red, I'm sorry, this is going to hurt."

She smiled at him, loving his gruff voice and his endearment, and nodded. Finally feeling a little confidence, she reached her hands up his body as she said, "I know. It can't be helped."

Kissing his lips, she moved her hands up his finely chiseled chest. Rane position his cock against her pussy opening and slowly pushed it in. It felt so good she moaned into his mouth. As he got further in Kirby started to feel a burning, stretching sensation. She squished her eyes shut and scratched him down his back. Rane's breathing slowed, and his eyes sparkled as he looked at her. She could tell he was grinding his teeth, and his muscles were all bunched.

"Are you okay? Do you want me to stop?" he asked.

She stared into his gorgeous face. "No, please."

Nodding, he said, "I'm sorry, sweetheart. I think this will be easier."

As he said that, he eased almost all the way out, leaned down to kiss her, then in one powerful thrust broke through her virginity. She screamed into his mouth, and he stilled.

"I'm so sorry, my little red." Rane moved down her neck, sucking and kissing.

His hands shifted to her breasts, massaging and caressing. Every now and then, he would lightly pull on her nipples. The fire started to ignite in her body again, and she experimented by moving her hips. Rane looked up and gave a strained smile. She smiled back, and he slid up her body, kissing her mouth again, and started to slowly move with her. Kirby glided her legs up his and wrapped them just below his tight buttocks. He growled into her mouth. Feeling more daring, she trailed her hands down to his toned arse, holding on as it tightened with every movement.

* * * *

Rane looked at the sexist woman he had ever seen in his life. Kirby's fire engine red hair was everywhere on the pillow, he brushed away a couple of pieces that were covering her passion filled brown eyes. Her lips were big and puffy, and her cheeks matched her hair. Moving down her neck, to her full, plump breasts, he couldn't resist sucking one in and giving a small bite. He smiled against her skin as she yelped his name. God, that was the best sound he had ever heard. She groaned and started to pick up the pace. He chuckled because he had been going crazy trying to go slow so she could get used to him. Kirby was so tight, and he was afraid he couldn't last much longer; nothing had ever felt so good. She was his little piece of heaven. Deciding she was ready for him to take over, he pulled her body up so they were chest to chest. His hands held her to his body as he picked up their pace.

Kirby panted his name out as she tried to keep up the pace. He sucked on her neck where he knew she was most sensitive, and she screamed out his name as she came around his cock. Finally letting go, pulsating into her, he bit her shoulder, and she screamed his name again so loud that he was sure she shook the house.

"Shit!" Swearing because he forgot to tell her about the lock, Rane felt his dick lock at the base of her pussy.

She moaned and bit his shoulder back. He cried out her name as he continued coming, feeling pleasure like he had never experienced before. Rane knew he could never feel this with anyone else.

As her mouth let go of his shoulder, she groaned and her head fell to the pillow. She was so sexy. Rane moved them to the side to spoon and leveled himself up to watch her eyes close. She smiled a secret smile, snuggling her body into him, and fell straight to sleep. Kissing her forehead, he laid on his back. Moving her onto his body, he wrapped his arms around her and fell into the most peaceful sleep he'd had since being a child.

Chapter 7

Kirby winced as she stretched to the morning sun peeking through the curtains. Moaning, she snuggled into Rane's muscular chest. She kissed his chest and got up.

He groaned, grabbed her waist, and pulled her back down for a morning kiss. "Morning, little red."

She smiled up at him. "Hi."

Not believing what had happened last night, even as memories flashed before her eyes, she ducked her head from his stare, mortified.

He chuckled. "Don't do that. There's nothing wrong with anything that we did last night. To my people, we are now mated, married as you would call it. Once we mate, we mate for life and there is no such thing as divorce."

Kirby's mouth gaped open. "What! How?"

Rane kissed her. "Tell me you are okay with this? I know I should have wooed you, and I promise I will explain, or try to explain, anything I can, but sometimes it's hard to and I forget that you're human."

Kirby stared at Rane. "Is there any way that I can become a werewolf? You bit me."

Rane grinned. "No, little red, you can only be born a

werewolf."

Releasing a breath she didn't realize she had been holding, she noticed Rane's face drawn in a frown.

"Not that I would mind, but I already feel weird. I don't know how I'd feel with that added on." She frowned as she remembered something that she had heard. "I was told that werewolves were 'long lived', and if I'm your mate and that means we're married, what does it mean by long lived? I don't want to be old and you still look like you do now."

He took her hand and kissed it. "No, you won't grow old while I stay looking young. It's kind of complicated. We live about one hundred and fifty to two hundred years—"

She gasped. "How old are you?"

He chuckled. "Only thirty-two. I'm very young for a werewolf."

"Wow! How old is Kane then?"

"We're all pretty young. He's only thirty-five, but he's the oldest child in the family. The whole pack is young. Tray is forty, and his family moved to Australia when he was two years old. Blake, who you seem to like," he growled out, "is forty-five. There are others who are older and came here with their parents, like Blake and Tray did. One of the reasons we think we live so long is because with

Page 82

our true mate, we produce the highest quality offspring. Although it's very rare, if we mate with someone our wolf knows is not our true mate, it never works out, as we are one with our wolf."

Kirby frowned, trying to take everything in. "How did you know that I was your mate? I remember you saying something about smell, but what else?"

He smiled and sniffed her, breathing her in. "Yes, you smell like my favorite things, apple and cinnamon. My wolf recognized you straight away, some say they recognize their mate from a past life, others say they look at their mate and know all, I think it's a bit of both. From what Faith has told me, and from what I've seen for myself this weekend and throughout my life, I know the true mate bond got it right. Don't get me wrong, I know we won't be perfect, but nothing ever is."

Kirby smiled. "Thanks, I think. I'm looking forward to getting to know you more too."

Kissing her forehead, he continued. "Answering your question...no, you will not grow old while I stay young. My biting you transferred something into you. I don't know what to call it. Faith says it's magic, and for the sake of this discussion, let's just say it is. So because of my bite and my penis locking inside you, and so forth, you will age at the same rate as me, heal quicker, gain extra strength, and have all around a lot more energy."

Kirby knew she must look a fool with her eyes large and a mouth that wouldn't shut, but she didn't care. Her mind raced with all the possibilities of these new abilities she would have, and she also realized that with Rane being what he was, he wouldn't be scared away by her family.

Snapping her mouth shut, she hugged Rane as tight as possible. "This is fantastic news. With your super strength, and now my added abilities, you won't be scared away by my brothers. For once, maybe I could win a fight, have a boyfriend. Oh, you could probably kick their arses for me and not even break a sweat."

He chuckled, which made his rock hard chest vibrate. Mmm, she loved his body.

"After everything I've just told you, the first thing you think about and are happy about is that I'll be able to beat your brothers up? And, little red, we are a lot more than just boyfriend and girlfriend."

He growled the last and pulled her lips to meet his. She melted into his embrace as his hand moved down her back. Pulling her mouth away from Rane's, she stared into his eyes. She had so many questions.

"Will I be able to run faster, or do you think you could

teach me to beat my brothers in a fight?"

Rane sat up, pulling her with him, laughing. "You are a blood thirsty woman."

She whacked Rane's chest, but he just laughed harder. "It's not funny. I'm serious."

"Oh, I know you are, that's what's so funny. You have just learnt that you're mated to a werewolf forever, and you'll live longer, among other things, but all that matters to you is that you get payback at your brothers."

She whacked him again. "What is so funny? I'm so sick of being picked last for every family sport thing. That's not the worst though, when I was younger, they always picked on me, and even though I have an animal affinity, I still am not a fan of stick bugs, mice, rats, spiders, and snails. Do you know what I would find in my bed all the time? I even woke up screaming several times to mice crawling on me, or bugs, but the worst had to be the two hairy huntsmen spiders." She shivered, remembering that morning. "They got worse as they got older. I never got to date, or make friends, as they were all terrified of my brothers."

Rane hugged her tighter in a lame excuse to comfort her, but it was lost on her, being he was laughing so hard. She whacked him a couple more times until he let go and she got off the bed. He was laughing so hard she didn't think he even noticed.

"It's not funny. You're acting just like them, and they're one of the reasons I left, so I wouldn't be picked on, and to make some friends, be independent, learn to stick up for myself against overbearing arseholes." Turning, she started looking for her clothes. All men were idiots!

* * * *

Rane tried to stop laughing, really he did, especially knowing Kirby was getting cranky and looking for her clothes. The problem was he and his brothers would never do anything like that to their sisters, but their sisters would, and did, do stuff like that to them.

"I'm sorry, little red. I'm not just laughing at how cute you are, I'm laughing because in our house it was the other way around, the girls would terrorize us." He grabbed her waist, pulling her back on the bed when she reached down to get one of her ripped pieces of clothing.

He pulled her into his body, but she remained stiff. He kissed her shoulder and up her neck murmuring, "I'm sorry. Please don't be angry. Come on. I'll beat up your brothers for you however you want."

She finally relaxed into him, looking at his eyes and giggling. "I don't want you to hurt them. The thought really only crossed my mind for maybe a second or two." He smiled at her, and she sighed. "Oh, okay, ten, fifteen minutes tops. Oh, shoot, fine, I'm still thinking it's a good possibility." He chuckled and she joined in, chuckling along with him. Snuggling closer into him, she rested her chin on his chest as she murmured, "I hate to say this, as I'm so comfy, but we should probably head back to Faith's and Kane's. I mean, the reason I'm here this weekend is because of Faith's birthday. I know we really haven't finished discussing everything—"

He placed his hand over her mouth, silencing her. He moved her off him and on the bed, telling her to stay for a couple of minutes. Without even bothering to get dressed, he ran out of the bedroom and to the front door, opening it before the two battered and bruised werewolves had the chance to open it.

Fuck, something major must have happened. They should have been healed by now. "Come in. What happened?"

Blake stepped forward. "You and your mate need to come to Kane's house now. We've called a meeting of every available werewolf."

Nodding, Rane went to get Kirby from their room. He almost forgot about the two werewolves waiting in his hall when he saw Kirby bent over in one of his black shirts that came to her knees. She seemed to be looking for her other shoe. "Ah, little red, if we didn't have to be somewhere now…" He moved up behind her, growling. She dropped the one shoe she had found and moaned as his hands snaked up her body. "Mmm, oh my, you don't have anything else on." He groaned.

"Well, if someone hadn't ripped all my clothes, then maybe I wouldn't just be wearing your shirt."

His groan turned into a growl as he heard the two werewolves outside chuckle. He rested his head on her shoulder, and then turned her around to face him. "Wear my shirt. It looks better on you, and I like more of my scent on you." Her cheeks blushed a pretty pink. "Don't worry about your shoes, I'll carry you."

"No, I'm too heavy. You ca—"

He cut her off by picking her up in a cradle hold and kissing her lips. "Don't ever let me hear you say that you're not perfect. You're light as a feather." She laughed when he lifted her above his head several times. "See, my little red, you are lighter than a feather."

She reached up and kissed him. "Let's go."

They all left the house and ran to Kane's.

* * * *

They entered a house full of chaos. Once they were inside, Kirby ran straight to Faith and Sara, who were crying. "What happened?"

Faith blabbered out, "I didn't see anything. I never saw anything coming. I should've seen it. They have to be okay. She has to be okay. I sent extra men later when I started to get a bad feeling, but we didn't really think they would need them. Who would think they would attack a bowling alley? They're going to be okay. They have to be."

Rane's mother Della came to Faith and wrapped her arms around her, whispering, "Faith, you need to calm down. Remember the baby. This is not your fault. You cannot see everything."

"But, she, she, he…" Faith blabbered out.

"Shhh, both our best healer and Kane are in there looking at them. You know he's the best doctor there is."

Kirby was starting to fret as well. What the hell had gone on? She needed more information. Looking around the room, she didn't see anyone else she knew. Where were Remy and Bengie? She finally saw someone she knew, one of Rane's brothers, Jamie. Walking over to Jamie, she tapped him on the arm to get his attention. Now, on closer inspection, she could see he wasn't in very good shape either. "What happened?"

He didn't even glance down at her as he stated, "We were at the bowling alley, all having fun. I never thought they would come to a bowling alley. There was no warning, no nothing. All of a sudden we smelled the sulphur and everywhere we looked there were fucking demons. Fifteen, I'm telling you, fifteen, they swarmed in with minions and zombies. There were only eight of us, that's including my sisters, Remy, and Bengie."

He shook his head like he was trying to dispel a nasty thought.

"Bengie, he… I don't think they knew his potential when they let him go and haven't come searching for him. He fucking kept three, and I mean three huge demons from Remy. I…we can't…can't…" He shook his head. "And wow, Remy wasn't doing so bad herself with minions, but once the four demons surrounded them, they just..."

He seemed to choke as he spat out, "Remy was amazing. She set demons on fire, burnt most of the minions that way. Demons are different to minions, they can take the pain." A tear fell out of his eye, sliding down his face. "It felt like hours, although I'm sure it was only minutes, when the stupid fucking police started showing up and shooting the demons. It made the fuckers stronger. Finally reinforcements came, but they weren't enough. Faith couldn't, Faith... She didn't see how many. We didn't know how many. So they only sent eight more and we really needed double. All of us fought as best we could until more help arrived, but with the demons enhanced from the lead bullets the stupid humans used..."

He glanced behind her, and she felt Rane's arms come around her waist.

"I'm sorry, man, one of your human army men is dead and one is in critical condition. None are as bad as Remy and Bengie." Tears were freely rolling down Jamie's face now as he whispered, "They're in real bad shape." Kirby could barely hear him as he said, "I don't know if Remy will survive this. We have had problems as we cannot chance a hospital visit, especially with Bengie. Remy's not..."

Faith jumped up from the lounge, Rane's mother let go of her. Her eyes turned an eerie color as she seemed to lose focus and yell out, "Call Arden, he has to come home, now! Call Arden, call him."

Everyone turned to Faith. Della touched her shoulders. "Sweetheart, he's not due back from his away team for three more weeks. They're in Canberra, and it will take him hours to get here."

"I don't care. Get him here *now* or I will never forgive

you."

Everyone gaped at Faith. Rane's dad came up and tried to pull her in for a hug, but she fought it.

"No, no, he has to come. She's his mate."

"Faith, she can't be Arden's mate. He would have recognized her, or said something by now. She's been friends with you for years. No, she can't be."

Sara spoke through sobs. "No, this is the first time Remy's been out here. We never understood why Faith never had sleepovers or invited us to her house for visits. Faith just never wanted us to, and Remy didn't come to Kane's thirty-fifth birthday party. We have only ever been around your daughters, Jamie, and Devlin, although recently Kane too."

Everyone stared wide-eyed at Faith. Her lips were pursed and her eyes seemed to be flashing with anger. "What? Stop looking at me like that. It's not how I envisioned them meeting. I saw it differently, but..." She looked at Jack and then at everyone. "They're messing with the future, so I don't see why I can't. If she dies, the future I saw will be out of whack anyway. All I know is she can't die." She glared at everyone in the room, before she added, "None of you can tell him, or her, why he has to come home."

Rane growled at the same time as his father and then everyone gave a reluctant nod. Jack slowly walked away with his phone to his ear. He arrived back only a minute later. "I told Arden he has to come home ASAP, family emergency."

Faith seemed to deflate. She grabbed Kirby and Sara's hands, pulling them down the hall. "Come on, let's go see them. They're in my poor brother's bedroom. He will be okay. They're all going to be okay."

Kirby didn't know what to expect. She tried to think on the bad side, so she could prepare herself for what she was about to see.

Remy was just one big, purple bruise. Her left arm was broken, her ribs were wrapped, and she was covered in cuts. One ankle was swollen, and she was either sleeping or unconscious—Kirby wasn't exactly sure which one.

Sara gasped and ran to her side. "How can Arden save her? Look at her."

Faith smiled at them both. "You don't realize how special you are, do you? Did Tray or Rane explain nothing to you?"

Kirby nodded. "A little bit about the bite." Whispering, she added, "The sperm and lock of his penis, that it will all help us to heal and live longer, and something about how the wolf chooses."

Faith laughed. "I'm going to let you in on a secret. You will never find an unmated werewolf over the age of one hundred. His life after so many years of fighting and killing, even knowing they are killing demons, minions, and zombies, their souls can't take it much more without someone to share the burden, or someone to bring some light into it. Can you imagine living that life and never having someone to talk to, laugh with, and love? Oh, they can mate with others, but it's not the same as a true mate, it's not their soul mate. Their savior, their light in their otherwise dark world. I'm not saying being a true mate is easy. Let's just say you were made for each other. You're a perfect match. Mating with their true mate will always bring the strongest children and they will always feel loved. It's also not just the magic that they transfer over, it's the unconditional love."

"How does this save Remy?" Kirby asked.

Faith grinned. "I'm so glad Arden is her mate, because this is going to take a lot of patience. He absolutely won't be able to have sex with her, because of the condition she is in, so he will have to just bite her shoulder."

"Arden will find a way to save her, trust me." They all turned, shocked to see Kane standing on the other side of the room. They hadn't noticed him until he talked.

Faith smiled at her mate, then grabbed Kirby's and Sara's arm and patted them gently as she said, "I'm really sorry, but after the incident last night, we can't take any chances. You're both going to have to live here, or with your mates. We just can't chance the demons getting a hold of you two. But don't fret. You are some of the luckiest women in the world to have men like this. You'll see." Faith nodded as they sat down next to her brother's bed.

Kirby glanced behind her to see Rane standing in the doorway. When his eyes met hers she could tell that he was troubled.

Faith seemed to change her mind and stood up. She grabbed Kirby's hand, dragged her over to Rane, and placed her hand in Rane's, then Faith sat back down next to her brother.

Kane turned to them. "Mates are on lockdown, everyone is going to have to buckle down. We can't lose any more mates to the demons. We're going to up our ante and find our mates before they do."

Faith kissed Kane's cheek as she said, "I know they're holding women that are mates to our werewolves. I don't know whose mates yet, but I think moving up our raid of the demons' hideout would be a good idea. I also think we have to train all of the supernaturals starting tomorrow, especially the mates as the men can't live long without them."

Rane spoke up behind her. "I already was hoping to have something like this organized. Devlin and Jamie will be perfect for that job."

Kane and Faith both nodded.

Kirby shivered as Faith went into one of her trances and came out of it with an evil smile on her face. "Ah, before you go, Rane, you will be getting ten more recruits from England and America. They'll be arriving in a couple of days, so make sure you add that when the Australian Army gives you the new amount." Rane raised his eyebrow and groaned as Faith continued. "Grab Kirby's stuff from her flat, she shares her flat. Pay the rest of her lease out."

Kirby stared open-mouth and dumbfounded. She seemed to be doing that a lot this weekend at everything that came out of Faith's mouth.

Faith paused and looked at her. The wicked grin never left her face, it just got bigger as she said, "Make sure Kirby goes with you to the military compound today. Go now, shoo."

Rane groaned again, tightened his hold on her hand, and walked as fast as he could with her running to keep up

Rane's Mate / Hazel Gower

with him.

"What the hell just happened?" Kirby asked.

Rane shook his head. "Yeah, she does that to all of us. She's freaking amazing like that."

Kane followed them and tapped on Rane's back to get his attention. "All your recruits will be here by Thursday. You'll need to prepare them as best as possible for the take down of the demons' stronghold."

Rane gave the slightest of nods before they left the house.

Chapter 8

Rane looked at Kirby seated in the SUV he had parked across from the entrance to the human military compound. He glanced out the window to see the work he had instructed to be done was being completed. More barracks were being erected. Kirby was the first woman to go into the human military base, and Rane didn't know how he felt about that. He was excited to show her what he did, but also hesitant for her to see this side of him. It was silly, he knew, especially as she had already seen him in tough guy mode with demons. But this was different. Here he was the big boss, the highest military ranking officer, and what he said was law. He knew his training schedule was brutal. He was a hard taskmaster. Rane didn't have any weaknesses here usually, but today, his only and biggest weakness would be there for them all to see.

Rane moved and turned his body so he could look into her big brown eyes. "In here, little red, I'm Major Rane, hard arse." Gently touching her face, he tucked a red curl behind her ear. "I will introduce you as my wife. Since they're human they won't understand the significance of the word *mate*."

He slipped a square cut diamond and ruby ring on her left wedding finger. She gasped, staring at her finger. Chuckling, he pulled her face to his to give her a kiss. She melted into his embrace, her arms sneaking around his neck. He pulled away, sighing, knowing they couldn't do anything when he was there to work.

"I've been training six military men, and there are supposed to be another six arriving today. After what Faith just told us, I'm sure there will be more. I am so sorry, but now that they're going to send more I'm not going to have time with just you and me like I wanted."

She nodded and smiled. "I'm from Singleton, you're either a miner or in the military. Actually, both my brothers are in the military. It was kind of a shock that they didn't follow my dad into the mine. But thanks to my brothers, I understand how it works. Well, kind of."

Rane smiled. Of course his mate would know the situation, she was perfect for him.

They got out of the car and he walked them straight through the gates and into the compound. She turned not far from his office and started to say something. He couldn't hold back his groan, because as she had walked ahead of him he had noticed how smoking hot she looked in just a simple pair of fitted jeans and a black singlet top. Her black lacy bra strap was sticking out of the top of her singlet, and her hair had fallen out of her ponytail. The fire engine red curls were falling everywhere.

Moaning, he pulled her to him and kissed her before he could hear what she was about to say, drinking in her sweet apple and cinnamon taste, taking deep breaths of her heavenly smell. Fuck! He had never acted like this before, especially in his military mode. He groaned again as he sensed two people walking down the hall toward them, two of the humans that he had trained. He tried to pull away, but Kirby moaned and pulled him closer.

He reluctantly pulled away from her as the two men came up to him and stood to attention. He turned to see Captain Lance and Lieutenant Logan standing in front of him. Slowly, he removed Kirby out from behind him, only to hear her gasp.

Lieutenant Logan grabbed her arm, and Kirby winced as he pulled her to his side. Shocked, Rane growled and lunged for the lieutenant. He vaguely heard Kirby yelling, "Stop!" The problem was his wolf had taken over. Rane picked the lieutenant up and was just about to throw him when he was startled.

In his head he heard very loudly, "*Rane, you better let go of my brother Logan, or I will never forgive you. Now!*"

His wolf stopped mid-throw, and Kirby's voice repeated in his head again. *"Put him down now."*

He turned to Kirby. "He touched you and hurt you. You winced."

Kirby sighed and ran her fingers through her hair. "Rane, he was shocked. He didn't mean to hurt me. Did you, Logan?"

He turned to her brother who was still dangling in his arms.

Kirby's eyes narrowed as she said, "Logan."

Logan still didn't say anything. Rane's wolf was telling him to throw the man.

Rane smiled, showing his lengthened teeth. He turned back to Kirby, and she raised her eyebrow at him and said, "Don't even think about it, Rane."

Damn, he wondered if she knew how good she was. Feeling Sebastian come up next to Kirby, he could tell the other werewolf was biting his lip, trying not to laugh.

"Rane, put him down. Let's go sort this out in the gym." Sebastian turned to Kirby. "It's nice to meet Rane's wife." Logan made a choking noise and started to swear. Sebastian then turned to Logan, grinning as he said, "Lieutenant, I would shut it if I were you."

* * * *

Kirby sighed as she looked at her stupid brother. The idiot should have some sense, especially when a six foot four, massive werewolf had a hold of him and looked like he was ready to kill him. You would think that he would cooperate, but not her brother. How on earth had he stayed in the army for so long?

She shook her head and looked at Rane. He did look scary magnificent. Oh God, she really was a freak, because he looked so hot right now.

He growled, his free hand coming out to touch her arse. "I can smell you. God, you smell so good."

She knew what he was talking about and couldn't help the groan that slipped out. It made the situation worse, especially when her brother moaned out, "Oh, great. Gross!"

He glared at Rane, which was kind of funny, because Rane hadn't put him down so he was still dangling in the air while they were walking.

She bit her lip, but a giggle still escaped. She coughed to try and cover it up. "Please put him down, Rane. For me, please." She glared at her brother. "He'll be on his best behavior. Won't you, Logan? Please, Rane, for me." She knew she had Rane with the last plea.

Rane sighed, and none too gently he dropped her

brother.

Her brother went to grab her again...idiot. Rane stood in front of her and said, "You don't touch her, or say anything that she wouldn't like. Got it?"

Her brother really was an idiot because he didn't say anything as they headed down the hall.

Once in the large gym, the doors were shut and Rane turned to her brother. "You may speak now, Lieutenant Logan, but keep in mind you will not offend Kirby. Do you hear me?"

Some sanity must have come back to Logan as he nodded, saying, "Yes, Major Rane." Her brother then turned to her. "What the hell are you doing here with him? I know you know what he is. How the hell are you here? You live thirty minutes away. I've been checking on you, and there is no way my baby sister is married or marrying him. So you better start talking." He was yelling by the end.

Kirby could feel how tense Rane was and the growling was pretty loud. She glanced at her brother and gulped, she had never seen him so pissed off. Clenching her fists and starting to get angry herself, she stomped her foot like a child as she yelled back.

"I don't know why you're so pissed off. You work with him. I'm old enough to date who I want and be married to whoever I choose."

Logan took a step toward her and halted when Kane growled. "Jeez, Kirby, I know you love animals, but you're not marrying one. For fuck sake, they're not human, and that's just for starters. How many goddamn years older is he than you? Have you seen yourself? You're frigging five-four, and he's a giant at six-four. There is no way Hayden and I worked so hard to scare off any losers or jerks who looked your way, only for you to end up with him. For Christ's sake, he's known as the exterminator."

Kirby couldn't believe her brother; she had never heard him speak like that about anyone before. She was mad at Logan and mad at everything. She squared her shoulders, reached over, and grabbed Rane's hand.

"I can't believe you, Logan. You of all people know what they go through to protect us, and yet you don't think he's good enough for me?" She couldn't hold back the tears any longer as they freely ran down her face. "I have never been so disappointed in you in all of my life. I'm twenty-two years old, old enough to make my own decisions. I'm ashamed to call you my brother right now. I will have you know, I am the one who doesn't feel worthy to be married to someone as wonderful as Rane." She laughed as tears still fell from her eyes. "As for his animal side, I love that part of him more than you will ever know."

Not being able to look at her brother anymore, she let go of Rane's hand and ran for the doors. She needed air and to get away from prying eyes. She needed to cry in peace.

* * * *

Rane let Kirby go. He would find her in a couple of minutes, but first he needed to sort out her brother. "You will regret what you have done to my little red. No one makes her cry and lives. Unfortunately, if I killed you that would probably upset her more, and because I love that woman more than anything in the world I don't ever want to do anything that will hurt her." He smiled and knew his grin was feral. "You're moving teams, until I tell you otherwise you are permanently on my team and my shadow. Have we got it, Logan?"

Logan looked at him, his eyes now wide.

"If I were you, I would think of a real good apology." He let his wolf shine through his eyes. "It better be a bloody good apology for my wife. I'll see you at fifteen hundred hours tomorrow, in this gym." He turned to Sebastian. "I need to go find my wife. We will be back, unfortunately, because I have lots to discuss with you. I need a better recap of last night, as I have been told that we lost one." He glanced at Kirby's brother, then turned back to Sebastian, continuing on, "Start him on the swords at 0400 hours tomorrow. Don't let him rest until fifteen minutes before I come. Kirby leaves for work at around one-fifteen in the afternoon so I'll be here at about one-thirty." He made sure that everything he had just said was loud enough for Logan to hear, he enjoyed pissing him off.

Leaving the gym, he went in search of his mate. He eventually found Kirby on the edge of the compound surrounded by rabbits, koalas, and other animals. "You do know that wolves like to eat rabbits, don't you?"

She smiled and wiped her eyes. "I'm sorry about my brother. I am surprised at how prejudice he is since he is here. I didn't mean to act the way I did. I hope I didn't embarrass you."

Rane pulled her up from the ground, hugging her into him. "You didn't embarrass me, and that brother of yours has no choice but to be here. He goes where the army tells him to go." He hugged her tighter, and using one hand, he gently wiped her tears away. "I don't care what he or anyone else thinks. The only person who matters is you."

Kirby smiled into his chest. "It has been an enlightening forty-eight hours." She looked up at him. "Is life always this hectic for you?"

Rane didn't answer at first, because he wasn't sure

how he should answer. He didn't want to say anything wrong and lose her. Taking a deep breath, he let it out, telling her the truth. "Sad to say, something is always going on. Does that bother you? We are born protectors, it's all we have ever known—protect the earth." Rane looked at Kirby and he wished that he could read minds. He couldn't help what he was, and he just hoped that she could live with it.

She snuggled into his chest. "I'm trying not to let it bother me, it's just such a drastic change from my boring, overprotected, quiet life. Don't get me wrong, it's nice to know we have people looking out for humanity. I just don't know if I'm as strong as everyone thinks I am."

Rane picked her up, plastering his mouth to hers before she could say any more. He traced her lips before his tongue entered her mouth, meeting hers. Her hands snaked around his neck and he groaned out. "I don't believe for a minute that your life was boring, and you are extremely strong, all you have to do is look at what you've gone through over the last forty-eight hours." He gently kissed her lips again. "You haven't gone crazy yet. I wonder if Faith knew how it was going to be with your brother."

Kirby laughed. "It makes a lot more sense now as to why she wanted me to come here with you." Sighing, she gave him a quick kiss. "I'm ready to go back now. Would it be okay if I have a private talk with my brother?"

Rane frowned. He knew deep down that her brother would never hurt her, but he didn't like leaving her alone with Logan when he felt the way he did. Rane was about to say no, put off work until later and go home, when a bruised Devlin called to him. Devlin escorted Major Samuel Black and General Peter Beal.

Fuck, it looked like the shit was going to hit the fan sooner than he thought. He stood to full attention, saluting his commanding officer. General Beal saluted back saying, "At ease."

"I would like to introduce you to my wife, Kirby Wolfen."

The general nodded at Kirby and then turned to Rane. "We need to talk in private."

Rane turned to Devlin. "Take Kirby to her brother, don't go far." Devlin raised his eyebrow and Rane made the slightest tilt to Kirby.

Devlin nodded. "Sure, come on, Kirby, you can tell me all about your super powers."

Kirby smiled at Rane and followed Devlin, laughing.

* * * *

They found her brother in the gym, sparing with a guy.

"That's one of the new guys we were sent," Devlin

said. "It looks like your brother is giving him a real workout."

Kirby grimaced as she glanced at the bloody and bruised mess of the man who was now limping out of the boxing ring.

"Yo, Dev, who is the hot redhead?" Devlin gave them a wolfish grin.

Her brother knocked out the guy who had just spoken, then turned to everybody else. "Everyone shut the fuck up. That's my baby sister." The blond he had just punched sat up and Logan went after him again.

Devlin intervened. "Kirby wants to talk to you, Logan, but I don't know if I should let her."

Logan changed directions, lunging at Devlin. "She's my sister! I would never hurt her. You need to keep your opinions to yourself."

Devlin laughed as he dodged her brother's reach. "It's not my opinions you need to worry about, it's hers and her husband's, your commanding officer. You need to calm down. If you make her cry or hurt her again, I don't think the fact that you're her brother will keep you alive. You will really learn what the exterminator can do."

Kirby had heard enough. Knowing neither of them would ever hurt her, she intervened, standing between them.

"Come on, Logs, just give me ten minutes, please."

Her brother sighed and walked away without saying anything, heading to the changing room.

Kirby looked to Devlin for help. "Do I follow him or wait? Is that a no or a yes?"

Devlin laughed. "Yeah, follow him."

Kirby walked into the changing room, making lots of noise so her brother knew she was there. She found him sitting on a stool.

"So, sis, how long have you known they exist? They are classified info. I only found out a couple of months ago."

Sighing, she ran her fingers through her hair as she replied, "Well, you found out before me. I had felt them before, only a few, one or two werewolves, maybe a different were, here or there, but I thought I was crazy. Friday was when I found out they're not only real but so are demons. Later that night I found out I can control minions. Do you want to know the kicker out of all this? I find out these beings, werewolves and were creatures, save the world, and I'm a mate to one of them." Kirby was getting pretty worked up.

"So, you're not married?" Logan asked with a smile coming to his face.

Kirby gave a frustrated scream. "You have got to be joking. Out of all of that I just told you, all you got was that I'm not really married." She couldn't help herself, she knew it was childish, but she stomped her feet several times and punched her brother.

She smiled when he winced and replied, "No. I got the other stuff. I'm focusing on one problem at a time."

"What the hell is wrong with you? Why are you focusing on that? Who I marry has nothing to do with you, Logan. You are not my father. Dad is going to be bad enough as it is. What's wrong with Rane anyway? He's military, just like you and Hayden. You work with him and he's teaching you how to kill demons. I never put you down as being racist."

His head snapped up, and he looked her in the eyes. "I'm not racist. They're not even human. My working with them wasn't my choice. I was chosen because I'm the best. Kirby, you're my baby sister and he's a killing machine, not to mention the fact that he turns into a massive wolf, and when he's in half-shift he's a frigging monster. So yes, of course I have some issues with my baby sister, who is probably one of the most sheltered people I know, taking up with a werewolf."

Kirby stared at her brother and sat down on the seat

next to him. "Well, it's nice to know how you feel, and you are right, I'm pretty much all of what you just said, but I have to grow up sometime. That was one of the reasons I moved out here, so you all couldn't be so overprotective and I could learn for myself what's going on in the world. Yes, he is a werewolf, but really don't you think it's kinda funny that I'm falling for one when I have an affinity for animals? And just so you know, if he wasn't a killing machine we probably wouldn't be here, because those demons and minions cause a lot of destruction and chaos. I, for one, am extremely grateful to them. I even intend to help."

"What! No way."

She held up her hand to stop him. "Let me finish. Look, if you really feel that way, why don't I see if I can convince him to get you reassigned, but I'm staying here. I am going to help and do what I can. I'm not giving Rane up. I'm going to give him a chance." A sad chuckle escaped her as she continued. "My friend said something to me the other night, which I think you need to hear. All werewolves and were creatures do what they do so you, me, and everyone else is safe. Just remember that they deserve love, fun, friendship, and a life too. Give them a chance." Getting up, she walked out to let him think everything over.

* * * *

Rane looked at the major and general. "With all due respect, we're not set up for that many men. I don't have the man power to spare to even think about training that many."

The general stood up and in a booming voice told Rane, "You don't have a choice. Last night was a major statement to us all, and another attack that took place in another very public venue. I've called back eight werewolves from other missions, and they'll be joining you on this force. The epidemic is getting worse. I've spoken to other packs and we will have one other training facility in Western Australia, as these seem to be the best location. From what I was told you've rescued the most supernaturals. You have a soothsayer, and your land is near water. We're donating all of our surrounding land to you for your help."

Rane frowned. "Fifty more is a lot to take on and train. The ones you sent three months ago still aren't halfway ready. We lost one last night." He turned to Major Samuel Black. "You saw what was involved when you came out that night. At a minimum, it takes two werewolves to take down a demon."

Major Black cleared his throat. "Well, it did only take Faith and I to kill one."

Rane growled, fighting his wolf. "For starters, Faith has been training with us since she was five, and secondly, she is supernatural and she's also mated to one of us. Lastly, she almost fucking died thanks to that stunt." He held up his hand before the major or the general had a chance to say anything. "Before you even start to think about giving your men some enhancers I have to tell you they don't help, there's always some kind of drawback. I know you think we don't know about you working with our blood and your secret tests. What we are can't be explained by science. Dumping these new recruits to train is a lot to ask given that I haven't had the time to train the others yet."

The general's brows creased. "You still don't have a choice. They'll arrive by the end of the week. You'll be receiving the new facility, and any help you need is at your disposal. We're also making it a priority to find the demons' underground operations. I have spoken to your alphas. We are also giving you an extra facility for the paranormal people and they will be given a choice to live close to you safely and help. As I said, you will have those eight other werewolves under your command tomorrow. Major Cullen will be your CO to work on this. I'll be back in a week to check on the progress and the new recruits. Send me a report if you recruit more werewolves, I will add them on and it can add to time if they owe us. Women are welcome."

Rane gritted his teeth, and they left without letting him say anything else on the matters at hand. Collapsing in his seat, he pulled out his phone and messaged his father to meet him. Shit! What they wanted was a miracle.

His father arrived ten minutes later in wolf form. After he changed to his human form and put the clothes from his backpack on, Rane told him what had been said and how he thought it would affect them.

His dad sighed, raking his fingers through his hair. "It sounds like we will have a lot of work. Together, I think we can do it. It should also help that we're going to have a larger pack soon. England's ten or so should arrive any day now. On an even brighter note, the extra land will be a huge help. Ava is going to come and organize things, get all the paperwork done, I think that would be the best job for her."

Rane nodded. Ava would have everything running smoothly. She was perfect for the job. "Have Ava start next week. These are the men I want if you spare them... Sebastian, he has already agreed if you give the okay. Tray, but he's in the same boat as me, except with Sara. Blake and Devlin. Alex and David, and I know they're young but the general said he would class it as their military time if they wanted. Jamie just got out of the military. He said he would come back and help a day or two a week. Lastly, I did want Tristan and Arden. Thanks to everything going on, Arden will be home earlier and in the same situation as Tray and I. Griffen is even going to help. So if you give the okay, with all their help I should be able to pull it off."

His dad sighed. He looked exhausted. "If they all agree I think it will work, and the people you named shouldn't screw up my away teams too much or the enforcers' squad. You need to find a woman to train all the females, but it can't be Faith as Kane wants her to start taking it easy."

His father's mobile rang, and Rane raised his eyebrows in surprise that he hadn't turned it off when he came into the room. His dad looked at the caller ID and put the phone on speaker.

"Don't listen to Kane," Faith said,

They could hear Kane talking in the background.

Faith groaned. "Oh okay, if it's important to everyone I won't teach the fighting, but I have the perfect woman who can. Although, I don't think Kirby will like it, just tell her to trust me. Sandra, call Sandra. Oh, and Leaf. Retirement is boring and his mate says he's driving her nuts."

Rane grinned. Leaf was one hundred and twenty-five years old and had come to Australia to retire, although he was always trying to be busy. He would make a great instructor.

Faith interrupted his musing. "Rane, don't forget Richard, he would be perfect with his sword and knife training. It also helps that he makes all the weapons."

Rane shook his head. "Faith, you are unreal, I really don't know how we got on without you."

She laughed. "I hope I remembered everything from my vision of the meeting you're having now. I'm having so many visions lately it's easy to forget something. And I have no idea what you did without me either." She laughed again, and it was nice to hear, especially with everything that had been going on. "Rane, before I go, how are Kirby's brothers?"

He chuckled. "There was only one and you obviously know how they are."

"Oh, well, I have to go now. You know me, busy, busy. Love you. Bye." She hung up before he could even respond.

Kane turned to his dad. "I hate it when she does that. Now I really feel on edge. Let's go, I need to be with my little red."

His dad patted him on the back and laughed the whole way to the gym-workout room.

* * * *

Devlin had taught Kirby some basic fighting moves and they were now practicing controlling her animal mind control. The werewolves were shocked and not too happy to learn she could speak into their minds and, as they had now learnt, control them. This scared them as they thought they were immune to stuff like she was doing and any other magic bar their own. She did admit it was a lot harder to control them than the minions. Sebastian had left as two new recruits had turned up, so while Rane was busy Sebastian took the job of looking after them.

Her brother still wasn't happy and stood against the wall, watching her like a hawk. It didn't bother her as she was having so much fun.

Devlin turned wolf again and she knelt down so she was face to face with him. This time they were going to see how far he got to attacking someone at the other end of the gym before she stopped him. They had also made it harder by spreading the men out to block her path.

Kirby stood up, took a deep breath, and nodded. Devlin was off. She focused on his unique thread and yelled, "Stop, freeze." He didn't and kept going, Devlin was almost to his goal when she finally caught the thread she needed. "Stop. Freeze."

He seemed to almost freeze mid-air pounce. Vaguely

hearing the clapping, she held Devlin in place for as long as she could.

The opening of the door as Sebastian came in with her other brother Hayden and another man broke her concentration, and Devlin unfroze.

She sat on the floor with a splitting headache. Devlin came over to her still in his wolf form and changed just as black came over her vision.

Kirby came to moments later in Devlin's arms, clutching at her head. Logan and Hayden yelled over the top of her, at a naked Devlin. "Hand over our sister now!"

She tried to block out the arguing and sighed in relief when she felt Rane. He came through the door and seemed to take in the situation before he roared, "What the hell is going on? Report now!"

As most of the men were terrified of Rane they all tried to talk at once, until Rane cleared everyone out who wasn't supposed to be there with one roar. "Out."

Feeling a lot better now that Rane was there, she sat up in Devlin's arms only to be snatched out of them by Logan, as Hayden got between her and everyone else. Rane went straight up to her brother and tried to get her, but her brothers wouldn't give her up.

Devlin broke the strained silence. "Rane, Kirby was

practicing controlling her animal talent. She was doing amazingly well, she stopped me several times. The last time we put an obstacle in her way, and she had to stop me before I reached the opposite end of the room and see how long she could hold me. Kirby held me for a good five minutes before she got distracted. I think she could have done longer. Just before you came in she sat on the ground, touching her head. I went over to see if she was all right, and she fainted. I was going to go bring her to you."

Rane nodded at Devlin, then turned back to her brothers and very slowly said, "Give her to me!"

"Over our cold, dead bodies! There is no way you're taking our sister."

"That first part can be arranged."

Kirby sighed. Oh great, another pissing match. She tried to get out of Logan's arms, because she'd had enough, and she had just used up most of her energy. It'd felt different to the other night when she used her gift. She didn't have the added adrenaline running through her like she did when she'd controlled the minions.

Gritting her teeth, she tried to get out of her brother's arms again. When that didn't work she tried interrupting, but she couldn't get a word in.

"You let my baby sister fight those monsters. What

were you thinking? If I have my way, you will never see her again, you—"

Okay, she had heard enough. Before Logan could finish, she screamed at the top of her lungs, "Shut up!"

She instantly knew she must have also said it into the werewolves' heads as all four touched their heads and stared at her in amazement.

Surprised it had worked and the room was now silent, she elbowed her brother. "Put me down now!"

Her brother reluctantly put her down, and she walked straight to Rane. His arms came around her just as her legs turned to jelly again. As she sighed and cuddled into him, he picked her up, cradling her, and kissed her forehead.

As soon as she was comfortable, Rane turned and headed for the doors. Her brothers caught up and were still going on. She groaned, which made Rane growl. He stopped and turned to face her brothers.

"I am taking my little red to my brother, who is a doctor. Do either of you have a problem with that?"

Her brothers gave a reluctant shake of their heads.

Rane smiled, flashing his canines, and looked Hayden up and down. "You must be Hayden. Lieutenant Hayden." Her brother nodded. "I'm Major Rane Wolfen."

Hayden's eyes grew wide. He glanced at Kirby and

took a step toward her.

"Ah, I see my name precedes me. This is my brother Devlin, you've already met Sebastian, and this is my father Jack. They'll explain what they can. I have organized two days leave this Saturday and Sunday as your parents will be coming and staying for a visit. You two will be at our house to meet them. Call them tonight, and tell them Kirby has been seeing someone. That way they might not be so shocked when they find out she's living with me. I'm leaving, taking my mate-wife, so if you have any questions, my brother or Sebastian will answer them."

Kirby gasped. *Oh my God!* What was he talking about? What had he done? She tried to get his attention, but he was too busy talking to her brothers. Trying to reach his wolf, she gave a frustrated moan as she came up against a wall. Seething, she crossed her arms over her chest, which is hard to do when you're in someone's arms, and came up with all sorts of ways to get him back.

He walked outside and placed her in the car gently. She grabbed his face in her hands, making him focus on her. "When were you going to ask me to move in? Oh, how about, when are you going to ask to meet my parents, so I, me, I, can organize it?"

"I want you with me, little red. You can't go back to

your apartment. You can finish our house this week. I'll let you choose whatever you want."

She raised her eyebrow.

"Okay, no pink or anything too girly."

She couldn't help it, she laughed. He was irresistible, especially when he was trying to please her. He got into the car and started to drive. Her mind was going a million miles an hour as everything started to catch up with her. "What am I going to do about my lease? What about work? I don't know much about demons, but sometimes I don't finish work until eight PM, and I know Faith almost always has someone to pick her up if she works a late shift. Am I supposed to work my life around the demons and all this now?"

Kirby was pissed. This weekend had definitely been an eye opener, but for Rane to assume that she would just move in and move her life around was too much. She'd only known him since Friday. She hoped she hadn't gone from one overprotected situation to another.

"Rane, I hardly know you. This is a lot to take in. I know I'm your mate, and last night was amazing, but I'm human. You can't just put a magnificent ring on my finger and say we're married, then call my parents. Don't get me wrong, I really want to get to know you. Just remember I only met you two days ago. I don't know if I'm ready to move in with you, or for any of this."

Rane parked in front of his house. Without saying anything, he got out of the car and walked into his house, leaving her sitting in the car like a fool. Angry, frustrated, and confused, she got out of the car, slamming the door, then walked into the house and slammed that door too. Kirby then went in search of one annoying werewolf.

Finding him curled on the bed in wolf form, she stared at the beautiful tree bark brown wolf. "It's like that, is it?"

The wolf lifted its massive head and whined, his big blue eyes pleading.

"No, I am not falling for that. Change back now, Rane." She stomped her foot, hoping he would know she was serious.

Rane changed back into a very naked man and still he said nothing.

"You're not going to say anything?" She waited, but he just stared at her. Screaming in frustration, she yelled, "Answer me."

He raked his fingers through his short hair and moved so they were only an arm's length apart. Seeming to let out a breath, he grabbed her and pulled her on top of him. He murmured against her lips, "I'm not really good with words."

Rane's hands crept up her back and around to her front, caressing her breasts as his lips nibbled at her mouth. Her body came instantly alive, on fire, burning with need.

Kirby's mind fought, telling her to stay strong, be firm, get answers, but once he had her pants off and his mouth plastered on hers, breathing life and fire into her, she lost all ability to think and her anger vanished. She promised herself she would get answers later, much later.

One of his skilful hands moved down to her pussy, exploring. He switched their positions so she was lying on the bed and he was hovering over her. Growling, he ripped her singlet and didn't even bother with the bra, pushing it down, which pushed her breasts up to him like an offering. He groaned as he sucked one extended nipple into his mouth, then switched to the other.

"You taste and smell so good."

By now she felt needy and desperate. "Oh, Rane, I love what you do to me."

She felt him smile against her skin. Kissing his way down her body until he reached her pussy, he then paused and leaned back. "You're so wet it's glistening," he groaned.

He settled himself between her legs. His tongue came

out and lapped from the bottom to the top. He growled, lapping at her pussy, making sure he got all her cream. Shivering, she held onto his hair, loving the noises he made against her, which made everything vibrate.

She needed more, wanted more. Pulling him up by the hair so they were face to face, she sobbed, "More, more, I need you inside me. I want to come around your thick cock."

Growling, he lined up his dick and plunged in. Screaming his name, she pushed up to meet him and bit him when he pulled almost all the way out and thrust back in.

Rane roared and pulled out. She moaned at the loss, but he moved her so she was on her hands and knees, spreading her legs apart as far as they would go. He moved over her, his cock hovering at her opening, teasing her. She panted. "Please, please, I need... I'm burning."

Rane buried his dick halfway in. "Whose are you? Tell me you're mine, tell me now." He thrust in, making her scream in ecstasy as he pumped into her. "You're mine, all mine. I will never let you go. Mine, say it." He pulled her up so her back was against his chest and bit her shoulder gently. "Promise me you'll give me a chance." He moved in and out. "Say you'll move in with me. Please don't make me live without you."

She nodded, just wanting more. Holding her in place, this time when he plunged in, he bit her hard.

Kirby shivered, yelling at the top of her lungs as she came on the best orgasm she had ever had. "I'm yours, Rane, only yours, yours. Yes, anything, yes."

He relaxed a bit and put her back so her knees were on the bed, but he placed her hands on the headboard, all the time never removing his mouth from her shoulder. Rane used one of his hands to hold her in place, and the other to play with her clit. Kirby could feel herself building again. Rane pounded into her, and she knew he was about to come. He flicked her clit and roared out his release, biting her again.

Collapsing in a sexual daze of satisfaction on the bed, feeling his penis lock, she shivered in ecstasy. "Mmm, once you go wolf, you will never go back."

He chuckled and wrapped his arms around her, kissing her tender shoulder.

Yes, she knew she had been tricked, manipulated, but at that moment, she really didn't care. Kirby felt so good right now, she wasn't worried about anything. Snuggling closer to Rane, she fell asleep, feeling safe and satisfied.

* * * *.

Rane knew what he had done was wrong, and beneath

him. But when Kirby had started talking about them not knowing each other and not wanting to live with him, he knew he would say something wrong if he voiced his thoughts, so he didn't say anything at all. Instead, he waited for her to get so worked up she wouldn't notice when he pounced, doing what he'd wanted to do since they reached the barracks.

He couldn't lose her. She was his angel, and he loved everything about her. He loved having her with him where she belonged and in his house, well now their house. It was nice to have someone he could talk to and who wasn't scared of him.

Laughing as she snuggled into him, he rubbed his hands up and down her back. It was so good to have someone willing to stand up to him and say what they felt without being afraid of the consequences. No one stood up to him, bar his father and his oldest brother. He might not be the tallest in the pack but he was the biggest body wise, which seemed to terrify people more. He smiled as he thought of his little red yelling at him earlier on, chuckling as he remembered her stomping her foot, which was the cutest thing he had ever seen. She was so tiny at five-four, his cute little redhead.

As he slowly detangled himself she moaned out "no"

and grabbed for him. Rane kissed her forehead and headed for the kitchen. He was going to make up for his deception. Maybe making his famous lasagna with mashed potatoes and veggies for dinner would cheer her up. Whilst she slept he also needed to check in with all of his brothers and do some paperwork.

Five minutes before Rane was going to wake Kirby for dinner she wandered in wearing one of his black shirts. She looked so sexy, her curly red ringlets falling everywhere, and her eyes still sleep dazed. He grinned, knowing she had nothing on underneath.

She ran her fingers through her hair and came to stand in front of him. "What's that yummy smell? It smelt so good, it woke me up with my stomach growling and making demands."

Reaching down, he kissed her forehead, murmuring against it, "It's my famous lasagna, mashed potatoes, and veggies. It'll be ready in about five minutes."

She smiled at him, and his heart seemed to explode. She was his sunshine, his everything, especially when she smiled like that.

"Wow, you cook? All my brothers can do is heat canned food, or re heat food."

Rane pulled her into his arms as he laughed. "Well, I

have nine siblings, my mother made us learn to help out. I think the only one in our family who doesn't know how to cook, clean, and iron is Jamie. But we have Faith to blame for that, because she did all his chores for him." He looked down as Kirby's face screwed up.

"I mean this in the nicest way—I'm surprised Faith ended up with Kane and not Jamie."

Rane smiled. He had wondered about that for a while himself. He let go of Kirby and wandered over to get plates and utensils ready and to set up the table.

"I don't know if Faith told you how she became a part of our family."

"No, she hasn't."

"When Jamie was eight, he saved her from some bullies. She then asked to see Jamie and Kane's wolf. Kane had come to check on Jamie, catching the last of the fight. They were shocked that a little girl knew they were werewolves. She grabbed Kane's hand and walked to our house."

"Well, that just makes less sense. If Jamie saved her, why didn't she end up with him?"

Chuckling, Rane continued as he put a plate of food in front of her. "How about you eat, and I'll tell you the story?"

She nodded and groaned as she placed the first mouthful of lasagna in her mouth.

"Even though there's a three year age difference between Jamie and Faith, they became best friends. I think for a while even Devlin was close with them. Don't get me wrong, she got along with my sisters too, especially since there's barely a year's difference between them. But it was always, has always been, Kane for Faith, although he's fourteen years older than her. Kane was twenty and was studying to be a doctor in the army. He would come home from being away and that's when you would notice the difference, she would become his shadow, never leaving his side. It was kind of odd when you think about it—a twenty-year-old with a five-year-old following him around—but Kane didn't seem to mind. He actually seemed happier when Faith was around. When I think of it now, it should have been obvious to us. A normal twenty-year-old man wouldn't let a five-year-old hang off him.

"Kane never played with the other kids, but he always played any game Faith wanted him to, even playing her prince and swooping down to save her from Devlin, the dragon, or Jamie, the evil warlock. Jamie never seemed to mind when she left him when Kane was home. And when Kane was around Faith also seemed to progress more in

Rane's Mate / Hazel Gower

controlling her visions.

"I once came in and watched them all together. Jamie was playing in the pool with our sisters. Faith was sitting next to Kane eating ice cream, slopping it everywhere. She was asking about bones in the body, and not just the normal simple bones like the elbow, but the finer bones and what they were called, what their connections were, and so forth. It wasn't until I got closer that I discovered it was what Kane was studying at the time. The next day he left to go back to university, and a week later we found out that he had gotten the highest grade in his class in that area that he'd been studying with Faith. It went on like this until she turned…I think about thirteen or fourteen, the teen years, that's when Faith started to get shy, and she stopped being his shadow."

Kirby paused with a fork ready as she stopped and asked, "How did she keep up with Kane's studying? All those questions should have been too hard for someone her age."

Smiling, he continued. "We all would like to know how Faith knows and does lots of things. If you were to see them that day it would have been clear, it should have been clear to all of us. When Kane would leave she would go back to Jamie. I think it actually helped, as it gave Jamie a break. I love Faith, but she was a pretty full-on child. In the end, it comes down to Jamie is her best friend, and Kane is her lover, mate, and all-around confidant. The next time Jamie, Kane, and Faith are in a room alone and you can watch them, do it. Then you will understand there has always been a gravitational field around Kane and Faith. When they're in the same room together, they're very rarely an arm's length apart. That's how it is with true mates."

Kirby nodded, smiling as she asked, "Were you ever one of Faith's dragons?"

Rane's smile grew bigger at her subtle way of getting to know more about him. "Well, I would like to say that I was spared, although when someone knows secrets they shouldn't know and threatens to use them, you kind of never have a choice. If I didn't care about what she'd learnt, then the waterworks usually did the trick and I caved. Most of the time I was away with the military, or training. I knew from a young age that it was the route I wanted to go. I joined straight out of school." He paused and made sure he looked into her eyes as he asked her a question that he'd been dying to know to answer to. "What made you choose to work with children when you have an animal affinity? Why didn't you become a vet or something similar?"

Kirby gave a shaky laugh. "Don't get me wrong, I love

children, and my job, but people already found me odd,
when for no reason at all animals would follow me around. I
thought that to be on the safe side, I would stay away from
any field to do with animals. My brothers may be arseholes,
but they stuck up for me against all of the bullies. And as far
as I know they never dated any of the girls that were nasty
to me or picked on me."

Taking in everything she had said, he thought of all
that had happened. He had noticed that Kirby's confidence
had started to get better, even in such a short time, and he
was willing to do anything to make her as happy as
possible.

"Now that you've moved away from that town and you
have new friends and a new life, if given the option, would
you change your profession?" He looked into her beautiful
brown eyes, waiting for her answer.

Her eyebrows furrowed. She pursed her lips and spoke
slowly as if she was thinking over every word she was
saying. "Truthfully, I don't know. I do love my job, for
now. I don't know what I would do if I did something with
animals. I know I couldn't be a vet, because I'm not good
with death or blood, guts, or anything like that." She put up
her hand before he could butt in. "I know the other night
there was blood and other yucky stuff, but that was different

then, having to operate or work on animals that you love is not something I could do. Working for an animal rescue or the RSPCA would really make the animal affinity show, as I would feel so bad for the animals, I would probably donate most of my pay and end up with a whole heap of animals at my house." She laughed. "I suppose I could be a horse whisperer, or work on a kill free farm."

He laughed too. "Well, that really settled that question."

She laughed along with him.

"So!" He tried for casual. "Do you want to go to your apartment and get your clothes and other things? You need to make sure you have everything you need for work tomorrow."

She only had a mouthful or two left, as her fork fell to the plate and she glared at him, shaking her head. "That was a cruel, mean trick you pulled earl—"

He put his hands up in the universal sign of surrender. "Please give us a chance, it's all I want. I promise you can leave if I do something wrong. I need you. Help me get the house ready for your parents. It'll be easier for us to get to know each other better if you live here." Her mouth shut, so he pressed on. "I really do need help choosing furniture. Ava got the stuff I have now, but she didn't want to get the rest, because she thought it would be best if I left it for my mate to choose." He reached over and grabbed her hand. Bringing it up to his mouth, he kissed it. "The biggest benefit will be, if you stay I'll get to wake up to you every morning."

Kirby sighed. "Fine. I'll call my parents from my apartment and tell them that I'm moving in tomorrow, give them the address and phone number, and have a talk to them." She raised her eyebrow as she added, "What did you say to them anyway?"

He knew he needed to tread lightly. "I told them that I've been seeing you for a while and have fallen head over heels for you." She groaned as he continued on. "I told them that I would love to meet them, as I have an important question to ask them. I invited them over this weekend, and they agreed to come."

She doubled over laughing. After a good five minutes, she straightened and said, "No, really, what did you say? Because I know it didn't go like that. It took me three years to convince them I was grown up enough to move away. They call me every day, sometimes more. I turned on my mobile before I came down here and it said I have twelve missed calls from them. So what did you really say, Rane?"

Grabbing her around the waist, he pulled her to him

and moved them to the lounge, sitting her on his lap and curling his arms around her. If he held her and kissed her, maybe she would be less angry. "Let me just start off by saying that your mother sounds really nice."

Kirby raised her eyebrow.

"Well, she did." In a softer voice he added, "At the start."

She laughed at him and snuggled in.

"I introduced myself and said that I had heard a lot about them, and that you were apprehensive about telling them about me as I'm quite a bit older and you weren't sure how they would react, especially with everything happening so fast. I told them I had asked you to move in and you had said yes. This is where it started to get…dicey. When your father got on the phone…let's just say that he is very creative."

Kirby was laughing so hard she was holding her stomach. "Oh, I can just imagine what he said. My dad makes my brothers look like pussycats."

Rane frowned and hugged her closer. "I kind of thought I might get a little sympathy?"

She stopped laughing. "You went behind my back, so you don't get any sympathy."

"Well, after some discussing of how long we had

known each other and that we had meet through your friend, your mother got on the other line and said her bags were packed and she would be here by tonight." He mumbled the next bit against her head. "I told them that your brothers were here and not to worry."

"Oh my frigging God!" Kirby laughed. "You had to play the brother card."

He grunted. "I invited them to stay this weekend, to see how happy you are. They still wanted to come, but I convinced them to wait until the weekend as we both work all week, and I told them that you are even helping out at the military base. What got them to agree in the end was that your two brothers will be here this weekend as well as my own parents."

She laughed again. "I'm the only girl, and there are seven years between Hayden and I, and eight between Logan and I. They tried for another child for years after Hayden was born, and they had given up when I came along. So I was Mummy and Daddy's little angel surprise. My mother was extra excited because I was a girl and I would get her gift." She giggled as she continued, "I always forget that she has an animal affinity the same as me. Mum's gift doesn't seem to be as strong as mine, but she is going to know what you are." Kirby frowned. "Do you think she'll know what you are, or be like me and think she's crazy?"

Rane kissed her forehead. He had forgotten himself that her mother or someone in her family had to have the supernatural ability for her to have one. "I don't know, my little red. I guess we'll find out on Saturday."

* * * *

It felt weird to be back in her tiny two bedroom apartment, and Rane made it feel so much smaller. His massive form looked like it barely fit in her room. Her roommate was at work, thank God.

"Does everything in your room need to come when we pack up?"

Turning to Rane, she shook her head. "No. Don't forget that you said I could leave your house if you stuff up. If I move everything and we pay the lease out, where will I go if you do?"

"You can always stay with Kane and Faith. You can never come back here though, because it's too dangerous, I won't let you risk it. Can you imagine what would happen if they found you?"

She gasped and took a step back.

Rane swore and came to her. "Look, I'm sorry. I didn't mean to scare you. I just don't want anything to happen to you. I need you."

He pulled her up so he could kiss her. His kiss started
out sweet, but as his hands moved down he cupped her arse.
They were interrupted by the phone as it rang and rang until
she couldn't ignore it any longer.

Letting go of Rane, she told him to chuck all of her
clothes into the boxes and she would sort them out later.
Kirby answered the phone, knowing it would be her parents.
"Hi, Mum."

"What's this about you meeting a man and not telling
us, me? Of all things." She groaned, as her mother
continued. "Tell me you're not moving in with him? Your
brothers said nothing. Really, all I got was 'yes, Mum, she
is seeing someone. Yes, it is serious. I don't know why she
didn't tell you, Mum.' So what do you have to say for
yourself, young lady?"

Kirby sighed. She had never lied to her mother…well,
the odd little blaming things she did on her brothers didn't
count, so really, she never had lied, and she wasn't about to
start now. She knew if she said even one thing that didn't
sound right they would be down here ASAP, so instead she
said, "Mum, I really can't explain everything over the
phone. Please be patient, I'll tell you everything on
Saturday."

Kirby rattled off Rane's address and phone number to make sure they were the same ones her mother had. She told her mum that she would speak to her tomorrow and assured her that everything was fine. An hour and a half later her mother hung up, very reluctantly.

Kirby turned to find Rane with eight boxes packed and stacked. "I haven't packed anything breakable, because I know how you women are about that."

Raising her eyebrow at the last comment, she added, "You women, really."

He put his hands up in surrender. "I'm sorry. My sister Ava can help you with the rest. I spoke to her while you were on the phone."

"Yeah sure, Ava seems really nice."

Rane looked miserable. He looked like an animal locked in a cage.

"Bored, aren't you?" she asked.

He grimaced and walked toward her. "There is other stuff that I would rather be doing, and this place is so tiny I'm starting to get claustrophobic."

She dodged his hands. "Don't start that or we'll never get back to your house."

He grunted and picked up four boxes like they didn't weigh a thing and walked out of the door. "Make sure I got everything."

* * * *

They arrived back at Rane's, unpacked, and were sitting on the lounge, cuddling and talking.

"How on earth are you going to have this house ready by Saturday?" Kirby asked. "The upstairs is just a shell with a roof."

Rane shrugged. "I'll have all the wolves pitching in. One of the best things about being in a pack is that there are always multiple people who have skills that you need. Most of us don't start in the enforcers full time until we're in our late forties, but some decide to do it earlier, it's their choice. We don't need as much sleep as humans. About four or five hours is all we need, unless we're hurt, and then we need more. Because of this most of us work and do enforcers as well. The mated werewolves are always given first choice of what jobs they want to do."

Kirby frowned. "That really doesn't sound fair, that means the unmated do more work than the mated males."

Rane shook his head as he continued. "Remember that we live a lot longer than humans and need a lot less sleep, so we rack up quite a bit of time. Most are not as lucky as me—they don't find their mates until a lot later in life. We also have a pack fund which helps everyone. When we pass onto the next life we leave a quarter of our money to the pack, and the rest gets divided between the family. Now, we are a new pack—we only started about thirty years ago—so it will take us some time to build up to where we want to be."

She nodded against his chest. "I suppose, but why so many different jobs?"

"We age so slowly that if we stay in the same job too long people start to notice, so we try to break up our long life. For example, Tray was a carpenter for twenty-three years. He even had his own company, but because he'd been doing it so long and never aged, he had to give it a rest and let someone else take over for a while. Tray is currently, and will probably be for the next couple of years, a full time enforcer. Then he will either go back to being a carpenter or start a new profession. Now that Tray has Sara, he could cut back and do part time, just work in the mines. He could probably have a rest from enforcer altogether, since he is newly mated." Rane stopped talking, looked at Kirby, and asked, "Would you like me to retire from the military and become a part time enforcer or take a rest from it all for a while?"

Kirby frowned at him, surprised he would ask. "What do you want to do?"

"I want you to be happy. I don't want you to be worrying about me, not liking what I do."

"I am proud of what you do to save our world." She kissed his nose and both cheeks before giving him a light kiss on the lips. "I also think it helps having brothers who are in the military."

He smiled as she took his lips to hers again. "I'm so lucky to have you, little red."

Chapter 9

Rane had two days to get the humans ready before he paired them with a group of werewolves for the raid on Thursday. This would be their first underground raid of a demon stronghold, and he needed them trained to save the demons' hostages.

Arriving at the military compound, he knew that he had to deal with Kirby's brothers first before he had to focus on his other major issues. Finding them in the gym, he smiled as he saw the worry on both of their faces.

"Follow me." He walked to his office.

In his office, he turned to them. They stood at attention.

"At ease. I know you're not happy about your baby sister being my mate, but I really don't give a shit what either of you think. The only person I care about is Kirby. Because she cares for you, I'll give you a couple of options. One—suck it up, or quit. Two—start trouble, and I don't advise this, because you would be surprised at what us animals can get away with. Or three—and this is the one I recommend—be happy for your sister and accept us werewolves into your family. If you choose the last one, there will be lots of benefits." He stared at both of them directly in the eyes. "What's your choice?"

They both stared at him, and it was Hayden who spoke first. "I'll choose number three."

"Welcome to the family."

"You better not hurt our sister, or you will be surprised at what we will do."

Rane smiled, showing his sharp teeth, and nodded, giving his full attention to Logan. "What about you, Lieutenant?"

Logan frowned. "I suppose I'm on the same page as Hayden."

Rane nodded. "I'll see you at my house this weekend. You're both dismissed."

They nodded and walked out.

As they were leaving, Rane added, "Lieutenant Logan, you will need to be ready tonight, you'll be with my patrol."

Logan nodded again and walked away. Rane breathed a sigh of relief. It wasn't perfect, but it had gone better than he'd expected.

He called all of the werewolves together so he could relay of the information that he hadn't gotten a chance to tell them yesterday. Eight werewolves squeezed into his office. After he had explained and told them all the important things, Tray was the first to speak up. "Fifty more men are way too many, Rane. Fifteen is way too much. We're struggling with the six we were initially sent, which is now only five. Yesterday we had another six arrive. We are too small a pack to handle this."

Rane sighed. "I said that. Their reply was they are calling most of our werewolves back from missions and so on. Which at the moment is only eight, but there are ten more werewolves coming from England's packs, they're going to be given citizenship on entry. They should arrive in a day or two, just in time for Thursday's rescue and destroy mission on the underground demon hold. It has taken us three months to get ready for that, and I'm still not sure we are. Not for a place like that."

His brother Kane came into the room. "You're going to have the humans practicing tonight. They're going to have to be thrown into the deep end. If we use all werewolves and do shifts of four to five hours hopefully we'll be ready for Thursday. I need them to know what they're getting into and what they're up against."

Rane looked at them all, not keen to tell them the next lot of info Faith had said. "Mates that have gifts can now be used against the pack, so if the demons capture mates, if they don't kill them, they can train them to use their powers against us. Faith says it's one of the reasons the demons are taking all of the paranormal humans, they are not chancing any of them not being our mates. We need to find as many mates as we can before the demons do, and rescue the ones they already have."

Just as he thought it would, his comment caused mayhem.

"Tonight at eight-thirty Sandra will start teaching self-defense fighting classes for all of the women we have saved, and any willing to join in. Faith will be here to observe Sandra's teaching skills." Rane sighed. "Speaking of the devil…" Before he could continue talking, Faith, Jamie, and Ben came in.

Faith smiled at everyone. Ignoring their chatter, she said, "Ah, I see I've come just in time. Yes, self-defense classes tonight for the women. I've come to tell you some good news, hoping it will pick up your spirits. By the end of the year over half of you will have mates, and all of them will be joining my classes."

All the werewolves talked at once again. Faith held up her hands just as Kane told everyone to be quiet. Kane looked at Tray and him. Rane got a sinking feeling as his brother spoke.

"Tray, Rane, your mates have to practice because

they're coming with us on Thursday."

Both he and Tray growled. "No fucking way. Our mates are not going into that much danger. There is no way they could be ready, no way are they going to demon central. No."

Faith glared at them both. "You don't have a choice. We've gotten them the next three days off work, and you need to get them ready. Kirby and Sara are quick learners. Remy is getting better, but she won't be one hundred percent until Arden gets here. The girls will come with us on Thursday, no arguments."

Rane gritted his teeth as Kane stepped forward. "Group one will be Faith and I, Jamie, Tray, Sara, Rane, Kirby, and Cullen. David and Alex have been moved up from the beginners. I know they're only eighteen and nineteen, but trust me, they are ready." Rane raised his eyebrow at his brother who nodded and added, "I've seen them, they really are ready. Four others are ready to move up too. Nathan, Jacob, Matthew, and Robert. I've told them to report to you and Blake. They should be here in about two hours. We need all the help we can get."

Faith rolled her eyes. "I told you they were ready."

Everyone groaned as Faith went into a trance for a minute. When she came out of the trance she said, "Wrath needs to come tonight."

Rane shook his head. Wrath was nighty-eight years old, without a mate, and too reckless. They were all scared they were going to lose him. Usually a werewolf didn't last past ninety without a mate, and definitely not past one hundred.

Faith glared at him. "You need to stop shaking your head. I just had a vision, and trust me, you're going to want to bring him with us tonight."

As he looked at Faith the whole room seemed to sigh in relief—their friend would be all right and would have a mate to help heal his soul. They hated losing one of their own. Faith started to walk out of the door then she stopped, turned, and smiled.

"Oh, I almost forgot, good idea, Rane, about Logan being on your team. Also, Bengie is going to start training with the new recruits. They need to see what kind of strength they're up against." As she passed him, Faith gripped his hand and went into another trance, smiling when she came out of it. "Oh, this will be good. I'll meet with the head women of the pack to talk about organizing a school and better facilities, that way the fifty new recruits will eventually be able to move their families here." Clapping her hands together, she rushed out of the door.

Kane shook his head before he turned to Rane and patted him on the back. "I have been told by Dad that I'll be here tonight to help with the recruits. Tonight I will show them no mercy. Rane, I want you to pull the cockiest one out of the bunch." Kane chuckled. "Faith is going to show him something, so bring him over as soon as Faith has finished the self-defense class." All of the werewolves laughed as he turned and walked after his mate.

Turning to the rest of the werewolves, Rane stated, "Training for an hour, and then I want them to have rest time, after that I want them to meet Kane and I." He turned to Devlin. "I want Hayden with you, Devlin. No mercy, let's see what he can do."

Devlin nodded, adding, "Those brothers of hers have high potential. I can tell you that from what I have seen." He chuckled. "It will be Logan who gets his arse kicked by Faith." They all laughed again and went off to their duties.

* * * *

Kirby arrived at Rane's at seven-fifty, surprised to see the exterior of the house almost finished. The door opened before she got to it, and Rane stood in the doorway in his uniform. Mmm, men in uniform.

"What do you think? I told you I would have it ready by Friday."

She grinned at him. "Wow, I didn't know it could happen so quickly. The finished product will be beautiful."

He pulled her into his arms, lifted her up, and kissed her.

Loving his taste, she moaned into his mouth. "I could really get used to this."

He pulled away, asking her how her afternoon had been. She walked inside with him, sat on the lounge, and told him all about her day. He hugged her as she finished off saying, "It will be nice to have a long weekend, although Faith told me what it's all going to be about tonight and the next couple of nights. I will be learning and helping. I'm so happy. This is going to be so exciting. This time I'm going to hold off all the minions."

It took Kirby a while to realize that Rane had stiffened under her. She looked into a hard, angry face. Sighing, she elbowed him. "What?"

Kissing her forehead, he murmured, "To tell you the truth, I really don't like you being involved in all of this. I don't want you in harm's way. I'm not happy with Faith right now. She's had training since she was six years old, but you haven't even been doing this for a week."

Kirby gritted her teeth and frowned. "I've been excited about helping. I thought you would be proud. For once in my life I feel useful."

This time he kissed her lips. "I don't like you in harm's way, and your brother will be there and I don't want him thinking I'm deliberately putting you in danger."

Kirby turned to straddle his lap. "I didn't think you cared what they thought, only what I think. Let me help, I really need to help. Please." She kissed him, and he groaned, pulling her closer.

"I hate agreeing to this, and I wish we had time to talk more about this, but it will have to wait until later."

They left the house, and five minutes later they arrived at the military compound for the self-defense classes. Rane kissed her and walked away. Smiling, Kirby turned to see twelve women, including Sara and Faith.

Faith smiled. "Now we can start. Remy would be so upset that she's missing this, but at least she can move now." Faith nodded and then turned to everyone. "We're going to do basic moves to start with, and then we're going to progress on. Three nights a week we will be doing this class." She looked at Sara and Kirby and said, "You two lucky ladies will be doing it every day. You are even lucky enough to be coming on Thursday's rescue mission."

Kirby smiled. It felt so good to be useful.

* * * *

Rane found everyone in the training yard. Kane was running all the recruits hard. He watched as all of the werewolves conversed about the good and the weaknesses they saw.

Forty minutes later Kane brought them in with a wicked grin on his face; it got wider as they came to the group of women. Faith, Sara, and Kirby came toward them, and Kane turned to the panting men. "What I have just put you through is child's play, but I will reluctantly say that there were a couple of men who stuck out, and I see a lot of potential. I'm going to reward you."

Kane turned to Faith and she came forward, all five-three, fifty kg of her, and stood next to Kane. She wore tight, leather pants and a matching top. Kane growled at the men as most of their eyes bugged out at the sight of Faith, and Rane laughed.

"Lieutenant Logan and Lieutenant Lance were by far the leaders of this pitiful group, but you two are still not up to scratch, and to prove this, so you don't get too cocky while you're out, Faith is going to bring both of you two to the ground. Now, I will tell you she is human with a bit of enhancement, nothing that should stop you two though, she is not military trained. She is what you would call werewolf trained."

Rane watched as Logan's and Lance's smiles became huge, especially as Kane continued on. "If you two can beat her I will give you two days off, and apologize for doubting you." Kane turned to Faith and smiled. "Faith will even agree not to go for the family jewels."

Faith smiled and stepped into the fighting ring that had been made.

Kirby moved over to Rane, pulling him down so she could whisper in his ear. "I'm not sure that this is a good idea. I don't like the look on my brother's face."

Rane kissed her lips. "Don't worry, little red. Remember what you saw Faith do the other night, just watch."

She smiled and then moved closer in to watch. Faith was in the middle of the mats, looking at both men, who were circling her. They came for her together. Faith laughed and kicked Lance in the stomach and punched Logan in the stomach too. She then spun, turned, and high kicked Logan. Jumping back, she kick-punched Lance, laughing the whole time as she backflipped out of the way.

Rane laughed too as Faith looked like she was deliberately playing with them. She sparred with Logan, and spun, flipping out of Lance's way. Rane could see the look of wonder on both men's faces. Faith used that to her advantage and pounced with everything she had, finally taking out both of them.

He heard Kirby murmur, "How does she do that? Move over Buffy." She chuckled. Kirby came into his embrace as Sara and her cheered. Lance and Logan had looks of respect and wonder as they sat up and stared at Faith.

She smiled at them, which turned strained a second later as she went straight to Kane and said, "They did good, but they need to keep their anger and frustration contained, because it's holding them back." Faith whispered something into Kane's ear before she fell into his arms and went into a vision. Rane took over from Kane, putting a human with every werewolf patrol group.

When Faith came out of her vision Kirby and Sara were sitting next to Kane. One held some bottles of water, and the other had sandwiches. While they ate, Faith talked to Kane, and his frown got worse the more she spoke. Rane moved over to hear the end of the conversation.

Kane looked up to him. "What do you want first, the good news or the bad?"

Rane ran his fingers through his hair, almost pulling it out. "Bad."

Kane's smile was strained. "We're going to have to

move our raid of the demon stronghold up. We're going on Wednesday. We'll leave here and travel through the night, arriving at daylight, so everyone needs to be ready pretty much now. Wednesday morning will now be D-Day."

Rane groaned.

Kane continued, "The good news, which we kind of already knew, is Wrath will have a mate by the end of the night, and she will be a healer. Here is a tiny bit more bad news. We're going to a hospital tonight. We're going to have a busy night, Dad is even coming to fight. We're pulling in every werewolf, even Granddad is going to help. He'll be doing locations, and Mum's getting the house ready for any supernaturals. We have four elders who are going to be drivers tonight. Everyone is pitching in."

Rane moaned, nodding as they all headed to the van where he saw an elder and Wrath arguing.

Chapter 10

As they drove through the city to their destination Kirby reflected back on the last couple of days. Had only been four days since she'd met Rane and found out about demons? It felt like years.

She couldn't believe she'd found someone who accepted her and her gift. She was so happy to be learning how to use her gift, fighting and helping save the world. She was mated to a man who was nothing like what she thought she would end up with. He was strong, stubborn, sure of himself, proud, and definitely a force to be reckoned with. Groaning, she realized that he was a lot like her brothers. If someone had asked her if she'd ever go for a military man or mercenary, she would have said 'no way'. Kirby knew how controlling and overbearing her brothers were. She didn't want that for herself.

But Rane had been more than anything she could imagine. She looked at him and sighed. He was way too good looking for her.

She knew he wasn't happy right now. His face was a granite mask of anger, and it was half her brother's fault, he had done it again, come over yelling at her and telling her she was not allowed to come out tonight fighting, then the idiot had turned to Rane, saying, "I can't believe you're letting her go fight demons, minions, and zombies. I thought you were going to look after her and take care of her. This is not something I want for my baby sister. I haven't worked so hard to keep all those military men in Singleton away from her only to have her fall into something worse."

What had shocked Kirby the most was that all Rane did was growl and nod his head. Kirby shook her head. She was pissed off with her brother, and Rane. Her brother should stay out of her business and stop being an arsehole. She was angry with Rane because he had agreed about her not coming. And he wasn't even trying to get on with her brother. You would think they would try as they worked together, but no, they couldn't even for her.

The twenty-five minute drive to the hospital was tense and uncomfortable, with only Faith talking, reminding Kirby she needed to focus on the minions and try what she had been taught earlier today. Sara was told to call on her water element powers and ice anything she could, with water to fire at the demons. Tray had gone nuts at that, saying Sara wouldn't be getting close enough to the demons to do that.

Sara and Kirby sighed in relief as they all got out of the

car when they arrived at the hospital, which was eerily quiet considering it was a metropolitan hospital. All the werewolves swore as the sulfur smell emanated around them, and Faith paled for a moment and turned, staring at Wrath.

"They've got her, Wrath. She didn't mean to do it, but she told them we're coming. She has no control over her sight, and only sees visions very rarely, but since she turned thirty she has been coming here to get help." Faith patted his hand. "I need you so enraged that you can take on two demons by yourself, because from what I've seen we're going to have to call in reinforcements. They have your mate on the tenth floor and—" Before she could get the rest out he was gone. Faith wasted no time turning to Jack. "Call in more reinforcements, because they are everywhere in there. They're waiting for us. There are about eighteen supernaturals in there, and over two hundred civilians. Once we step in they will be on us."

Faith turned to Sara and her. Kirby gulped, knowing what Faith was going to say. "I don't care, I'm helping," Sara and her said together.

Logan, Tray, and Rane jumped in with, "No, there are too many of them. Someone needs to drive the women back now."

"Don't even think that I'm not helping," Kirby said. "For once my power will have some use."

Sara added, "Think of all those people. That could be me in there, Tray. I'm a nurse, I'm going to help."

They took Faith's hands, pulled out their iced knives, smiled at each other, and were about to go inside when Rane grabbed her arm.

"Little red, I really think you need to go back. You haven't had enough training. Two days of training is nothing. Come on, not tonight, you're already coming on Wednesday." He kissed her hand.

Her brother piped up. "I agree with the dog."

Rane growled, and she turned to them both. "I'm going."

Faith smiled. "Kirby, minions will be the first things that come at us, so you'll need to be in the front line." Kirby straightened her shoulders and took several calming breathes while Faith continued. "Logan, I'll need you at the back to shut and lock the doors. I don't want anyone coming in." Faith then raised her eyebrow at Logan, saying two words, "Use it."

Kirby shook her head at the odd comment, while she felt Rane's arms come around her as he leaned down and whispered, "I'm really not happy right now. Promise me that you will try not to be a hero, because back up is a good half hour away, and I will personally tan your butt if I find out you didn't hide from the demons." He turned her and kissed her forehead. "Don't let anything happen to you. I need you, little red."

They walked into the empty emergency room. The smell of blood was so strong not even the disinfectant smell drowned it out. Kirby could hear faint screaming and moaning. Everyone started to spread out.

Faith shook her head and said, "Not here. Up."

They took the stairs. As they reached the second floor, Kirby turned back to all of them and whispered, "I feel hundreds of minions."

As they got closer to the door, the crying, screaming, and moaning got louder. Kirby was terrified, but she knew that she had to do this. Wiping her hands on the leather pants that she had been given, she stared at the door that would lead them all into chaos and ordered herself to focus on the minions. She nodded as the door opened and she zoned in on the first forty minions that came for them.

Focusing on as many as she could, she screamed, "Stop!"

Over half froze, but the rest kept coming. Never giving up, she kept trying to contact as many as she could. Faith moved, crouching down in front of her, getting everything that came at her head on. Jamie and Rane were on either side of her, with Logan at her back.

* * * *

Rane was amazed at his mate as she held twenty something minions back. Knowing they had to act fast, he, Jamie, and David, who he had to admit he was impressed with, backflipped in the air, taking out as many minions as they could. Moving forward, they searched out demons.

Rane dared not look back as Jamie, Faith, and Kane took care of a massive demon coming for Kirby. He ran down one of the halls where the screaming was the loudest.

A demon held two people, one was a woman in her late thirties, the other a man who seemed to be in his forties. The demon was looking into the man's eyes, and then he drank his blood. The woman screamed and the air around them swirled, moving things, making things fly through the air at the demon; the woman was an air element. The demon shook the woman and growled. "Stop or I will kill him."

The demon shook the woman again before his head came up and he stared at Rane. He wasn't the largest demon, only about eleven feet, although he had two tails, which was something Rane had rarely seen. It added to the problem, as the tails were like extra sharp hands with pointed arrows at the end.

Rane nodded to David, telling him to hurry as they needed to get up to the tenth floor and help Wrath. "David, you deal with the front. I will do the back."

Nodding, David attacked the front, cutting off one of the demon's hands with his long knives, which released the dead man, and the woman slowly tried to crawl away. Rane went for the tails, getting rid of them first, as they had the best movement and did a lot of damage.

Blocking as one tail came at him, Rane sliced the other off. The other tail tried to wrap around his waist, succeeding when minions came at him, slicing his skin and obscuring his vision with their body and wings. With the demon's sharp tail wrapped around his waist, its arrow head digging into his stomach, Rane killed the minions. He sliced off the tail around his waist, pulled out the arrow head that had embedded in his skin, and jumped on the demon's back. The demon bucked, growled, and threw his huge body around, trying to get him off.

The demon said, "You will all die tonight. We have over thirty demons to your pitiful numbers. You puny werewolves will all die," he spat at David. "We demons will have your mates and all the others that are here."

The demon grabbed David and threw him at the wall,

then banged his back with Rane on it against the other side of the wall. Using the wall as leverage, Rane pushed the rest of the way up and wrapped his arms around the demon's neck, slicing his head off. He then pushed the demon's body forward with his feet.

Letting David handle the rest, he ran, heading for the next level. Passing more demons and helping fight them, he stopped when he saw his mate commanding minions to freeze. A zombie came up to Kirby, and Rane glanced around, noticing that everyone was busy. He ran over to his mate, killing the zombie.

Kirby chanted "Stop, stop, freeze, freeze" over and over again. Faith and Kane were fighting a demon together only metres away from her, and Logan was killing as many minions as he could that were frozen. Rane helped Kirby again as another zombie came out of nowhere and grabbed her around the waist, which made her lose her concentration. The minions came out of their freeze, and they attacked. She kicked and punched and slashed at wings and cut heads off the minions, doing her best. Rane growled, trying to get the minions' attention and to get them to turn to him.

Logan turned at his growl, yelling at him. "About fucking time. Kirby needs your help!"

He growled louder as he used his claws to rip wings and grab at minions, pulling their heads off, roaring when a demon came out of the elevator with more minions and went straight for Kirby. Running to get to them before they reached Kirby, he backflip-kicked to get where he needed to be.

* * * *

Kirby was high on adrenaline. She knew in the back of her mind that when this was over she'd be in a shitload of pain and have one severe headache. She just couldn't believe what she had done, and what she was doing—using her powers to help kill. She didn't really care too much for the ugly creatures, but it still didn't feel right using her powers like this.

The things she hated the most though were the zombies, as they had once been human, and when they grabbed her she hesitated, which cost her. When she heard Rane's roar, she knew he had come to help her, and he would save her. He looked breathtakingly amazing, an avenging angel even in his half-changed form. The elevator doors opened and inside was the biggest demon she had ever seen. He was squished into the elevator, and when he finally unraveled himself he was easily seventeen to eighteen feet tall. She had no idea how he had even fit into the elevator, because she would swear that he was bigger than it was. She gulped as minions flew from the doors of the elevator somehow.

Faith came up beside her, swearing, and yelled over her back at Kane. "Hurry the fuck up." Then she turned back to Kirby. "You have to focus and gain as much control of the minions as you can. The less minions there are, the easier it is for us to fight the demons."

Kirby nodded, focusing on the new minions that were looking directly at her. These minions seemed to fight more, they didn't stop when she said, "Stop, freeze, stop!"

Going into their heads further, she noticed a scary thing, this demon was onto her, he was counteracting her. Knowing her friends were in trouble and that what she was about to do was stupid, she did it anyway. Searching for the link the demon had to the minions, she found it and stopped the minions.

Logan killed as many as he could. He came from behind her and moved in front of her. She focused on the link, but the demon started to notice and grabbed the link, laughing into her head. She fought as he told her, "Come to me. Kill the wolves. Kill, kill, kill."

Kirby screamed as the demon came closer and his long tail wrapped around her. Faith was trying to get around to the demon's back. Rane and Kane were fighting the demon from the front as best as they could, even as minions flew at them, but the demon's horns on his head were so big and he used them on Kane as much as he could. Faith was climbing up his back while Rane distracted him, slashing at him and trying to go for his heart.

Kirby struggled with the tail as they fought. Getting a good grip on her knife, she used it to chop the demon's tail from around her waist. She yelled at her friends as she caught some threads of the demon's thoughts. He was going to smash Faith against the elevator doors. Kirby yelled to try and get the demon to look at her, to get its attention, as she leaped through the minions, killing them and the connection. Kirby lost the demon's train of thought, but she didn't care as she now had his full attention. Rane freaked at that, roaring, finally getting at the demon's heart as talons from the demon's hands wrapped around Rane's middle, trying to pull him away. Without thinking of the consequences, Kirby ran up, using her knife to slash at the demon's arms. Her brother pulled her away as the demon's head rolled by her.

Rane turned to her, and she gulped. He was scarier right now than the demon. Rane nodded to Logan and then turned back to her and said, "Never do that again, Kirby."

She frowned as they walked to the stairwell. Very quietly and hesitantly, she said, "I was connected to his mind, through the minions, he was blocking me and when I got the thread it caught me and he was trying to get me to do things. I didn't, I just kept following the link from the minions. He was going to slam his back against the elevator doors while Faith was on him, so I acted without even thinking. I ran and I lost his train of thought because Logan and I killed the last minions. I don't know what the demon saw in my mind, I don't think he saw anything, but based on what I saw in his, I knew I had to help."

Rane and Kane swore, but Faith nodded and said, "We're going to have to look into that, I wonder..." She was cut off as the whole hospital started to shake. Faith continued, "Quick, we need to help. There is an earth element here." Faith cocked her head. "Maybe an earth witch."

Chapter 11

Two and a half long hours later, Kirby sat in the hospital's large conference room with twenty werewolves, fifteen military men, Sara, Faith, and another woman who was sobbing in Wrath's arms. The giant werewolf was gently kissing her forehead and seemed to be whispering calming words.

Two military men, who she guessed were pretty high up, called for quiet, but nothing happened in the room until Kane whistled then said, "Quiet now." His tone was so deadly she thought some men even stopped breathing.

The general stepped forward, introducing himself, and then started talking. "After tonight you have our full cooperation. We will help on Wednesday, giving you anything you need to find the tunnels and weed them out. I think we need more than fifty soldiers trained."

Rane cut the general off. "With all due respect, General Beal, fifty is already too many. We need all the wolves to be focusing their energy on fighting demons, not helping train humans. We don't have enough wolves to go around as it is, and we're doing things we have never done before. We're letting our mates help, plus—"

The general cut him off this time. "We need to protect and help in the fight too, today demons and minions killed just under a hundred, and wounded many more. The men you have so far seem to be doing fine."

Kane growled and took a step toward the general as the general continued. Kirby giggled as the idiot worsened his situation as he gestured to her and Sara.

"If the women over there can fight and win, then I don't see a problem." He pointed at Kirby. "I know you're human. You're Lieutenant Logan's sister." He raised his eyebrow. "And Rane's wife."

This time Logan growled too, and Rane seemed to force out, "Tread lightly, General. I shouldn't have to tell you this as it's not information you need to know, but the reason these women can do this is because they're supernatural in some way."

Kirby sighed as the idiot general then turned to her and said, "What are you? What kind of supernatural?"

Her brother came to her side. Rane lunged at the general, only to be held back by Jamie and Devlin.

Her brother spoke before she could. "With all due respect, sir, that's not something she has to divulge."

The general frowned and stepped toward her, which caused Rane to go nuts, and his brothers looked strained holding him.

"I looked into your family file, Lieutenant Logan Brown, and she has had no defense training. How on earth did she come out of this blood bath? She must have an extraordinary supernatural talent."

Kirby shivered as she looked into the calculating eyes of the general, who stared back at her. She straightened her tired and aching shoulders, so she didn't feel so small. Rane was let go and came straight to her side.

A pissed off Faith came charging up to the general, pointing at him. "Don't even think about it! You would be dead before you reached the door. Only the men you brought with you would fight, and I don't even think they would if you do what you are thinking of."

The general seemed to debate something and looked at Faith for a couple of seconds before he took a step toward her.

Faith continued. "I will kill you before you take another step."

This time the general raised an eyebrow at Faith, and his mouth turned to a smirk.

Major Black, who had been sitting quiet in the corner, spoke up. "Sir, I have seen this woman in action. Do not underestimate her. She's the woman in the reports who saved me."

Kirby could see the shock and the calculating glance that then came into the general's eyes. All the werewolves in the room were growling now.

Faith ignored them all and kept going. "Nothing would show up in my blood or Kirby's. If you're thinking that way, you aren't any better than the demons."

The general's face was red with anger as he looked around the room. No one supported him, even the men he brought looked at him with disgust. Logan now joined Rane as they stood next to her.

The general cleared his throat as he took one last look around the room at the werewolves. "I'll clear this mess up, deal with the media and all of the survivors."

Kane seemed to growl out as he stood in front of Kirby and Faith. "We will be taking any of the survivors who want to come with us. Some of the supernaturals will feel safer. We have been cleared for this already."

The general's face, if at all possible, seemed to get redder. He nodded then turned and walked over to his men.

Faith turned to them. "We have to keep our eyes on him. I agree we have to step up our training of the women, and make sure our women are never alone with him." She paused and made sure she looked at all of the werewolves.

"Now that I think about it, keep all of the supernaturals away from him."

All the werewolves nodded.

Frowning, Kirby said, "I thought he was the top ranks of the military and had all the power?"

Rane kissed her forehead before answering. "He is very powerful, little red, but he's not the top, although he is very close." He whispered the rest. "They don't know the head honcho is a werewolf."

Raising her eyebrow, she gasped out, "How do they not know?"

Rane shrugged. "We've been hiding from the beginning of time."

"You would think that we'd know by now that you guys existed. With all of this new technology, it doesn't make sense."

Faith giggled at her, adding her own two cents. "Normal people see and think what they want to. There has been video footage, but normal humans don't want to think of what is out there. They're all too involved in their own lives."

Kirby thought that through, then nodded her head, saying, "I felt you out there but I chalked it up to various things."

Kirby didn't even notice that all the werewolves, herself, Faith, and Sara had walked out of the hospital, until they were standing outside by the large tent that was the makeshift hospital.

"Della and Ava have spoken to the supernaturals, and it looks like they're all coming with us," Faith said. "Kirby, I think that we should go around tomorrow at lunch time and meet these new people, have a talk with them."

Kirby liked the idea, but now that the adrenaline was wearing off she was too tired to talk, so she agreed by nodding. Without realizing it she had been leaning on Rane more and more, so much so that she didn't think she had really been walking. She gave up on the pretense and leaned all of her weight on him, almost collapsing into him. Rane chuckled, kissed her forehead, and picked her up.

She smiled as she heard, "Thank God, I didn't want to be the first to show how exhausted I was."

Kirby didn't want to admit it either, but hurt too much to care who caved first. Sara fell into Tray's arms.

It was Jamie, who she had completely forgotten about, who said, "Think how the regular human military men feel. You have extra strength and healing, thanks to mating one of us. It's one of the reasons we haven't trained humans to do this until now, and the only reason we're doing it is because we have no choice."

That brought her back from almost falling asleep in Rane's arms. She looked around and asked, "Where is my brother?"

She couldn't see Logan. She did notice that the werewolves didn't even seem tired. A lot of them were leaving.

Rane whispered in her ear. "They're going patrolling. Don't worry, I've sent Logan back to the base. He's been with us all this time, while the others were only there for the last hour. We had already been there fighting for over an hour." He kissed her forehead again and sighed. "I hate to admit this, but Logan did really well, although he's pretty beat up and it will probably take him a couple of days to get back to one hundred percent. We're going to need him for Wednesday."

Kirby nodded into his chest, too tired to respond. He placed her in the car and gently kissed her lips.

* * * *

Rane woke the next morning at six o'clock, which was a good hour later than he usually woke. He'd slept in. He shut his eyes and took a deep breath, wrapping his arms around the lush, naked woman next to him and pulling her even closer. Rane chuckled as he remembered getting Kirby out of her clothes last night, she had moaned out, "Don't make me do anything please, I'll be good. Give me five minutes more sleep."

When she was naked, he'd placed her in bed, and as he walked away to do some work she moaned. "No, don't leave. You're so warm."

Rane had chuckled and forgotten about the work that needed to be done. He got naked and hopped into bed, and she had snuggled into him, muttering, "Mmm, smells so good, so soft and warm."

She hadn't made another noise after that, falling straight back to sleep. Looking at her now, she was gorgeous, her bright, fire engine red hair was everywhere, and he brushed a curly lock off her face. Her cheeks were a healthy pink, and her lips were slightly parted. His eyes drifted down. The sheet had fallen to her waist, and her breasts were pressed against his chest, the pink nipples pointed as the morning air hit them.

Kirby sighed in her sleep, snuggling into him more. He smiled, because he felt so happy and content—the best he had ever felt. He loved waking up with his little red on him. It was his idea of bliss. Rane knew he was lucky to have found her. She was strong, stubborn, and brave. One of the things he loved most about her was she was always thinking of others. Kirby was never afraid of him. She always stood up to him and didn't let anyone walk all over her. All the women he knew, bar his sisters and mother, never questioned him or would be game enough to say no and argue with him, they would never even dare walk away from him. Kirby was perfect for him. Rane couldn't have imagined someone like this for himself.

He smiled as Kirby rubbed her body all over him, moaning as she trailed her fingers up and down his chest. She leaned in and started kissing his chest.

"Please tell me the crews that are working on the house aren't going to start at six-thirty again. I need the hot water and power. I want to sleep in until at least nine o'clock." Kirby groaned out against his chest.

Chuckling, he moved his hands down her body, lifting her so she could give him a morning kiss. "Morning, little red."

Kirby moaned into his mouth as his tongue met hers. She lifted her hands and ran her fingers through his hair. He laughed as she mumbled against his lips, "God, I love waking up to a hot, naked, turned on man."

Rane moved her over the object she moaned about. She turned bright red and groaned.

"Please tell me I said that in my head and not out

loud."

He laughed again and pressed his rock hard cock against her. He breathed in her scent. The apple and cinnamon was stronger than it had been since he'd met her. It was filling his head and blocking all his other senses. Rane's wolf was prowling in his head.

Kirby rubbed herself all over him moaning, groaning. She didn't seem to be able to get enough of him. She licked, sucked, and raked her nails down his body. Her smell intensified, and he could feel her wetness against his body.

His penis was the hardest it had ever been in his life. Kirby moved her hands down, rubbing his dick with her smooth, soft hands, which were barely able to close around it. He couldn't take any more, and he finally snapped.

Pulling her mouth back up to his, she growled, pushing him back against the bed with the strength only a full-blooded shifter should have. He howled, grabbed her waist, and placed her over his dick. She fought, fighting for control and dominance.

Growling, his little red shoved his hands off her waist, positioned her pussy over his cock, and slowly moved down until his cock filled her completely. She screamed with a look of ecstasy as she raked her nails down his chest.

Her scent kept getting stronger, assaulting his every

breath. Her pussy muscles clamped tightly around his dick. He was sweating, telling himself not to come like a teenage boy with his first woman.

In the very back of his mind, he remembered one of the elders and his parents telling him the signs of a woman in mating heat. Fuck! His little red was in heat. Shit! He knew he had to say something, because if they continued, she would end up pregnant. He needed to stop now or use something to prevent it.

It wasn't that he didn't want Kirby to be pregnant, he just didn't want to be like his brother Kane and take her choices away...ever.

Blocking the heavenly smell as best he could, he growled out through clenched teeth. "Kirby, you need to stop and listen to me."

She froze as soon as he said her name. "You never call me by my name."

He chuckled. His mate was in heat, and the only thing that stopped her was him using her given name. "You need to listen to me, Kirby, you are in heat."

She growled back. "I know. You make me so hot."

"Kirby, focus. No, I mean in heat like an animal. Like a female werewolf. If we make love today, or while you're in heat, without protection of some sort, you will get pregnant."

"God, I love your lips, I want your lips wrapped
around one of my nipples or on my pussy." She moaned and
moved up and down his cock. He groaned as she continued.
"Mmm, I don't know what I want, your cock makes me so
full, but when you put your mouth on me…ahhh, ohhhh."

Rane closed his eyes, fighting his wolf like he'd never
had to in all his life. He needed her to trust and love him.
Rane didn't want his little red to wake up later, angry with
him, and leave him when she came to her senses.

Grabbing Kirby to still her, he ground out, "Listen,
because I am on my last thread of control." He reached up
and held her head down to his so their eyes met. "Kirby, if
we have sex right now, you will get pregnant and have a
baby in seven months. Do you understand?"

She seemed to come back to him for a moment. "Seven
months? A baby takes nine."

"When I bit you, and from our first exchange of body
fluids, I made you part werewolf. Remember I told you
about the extra strength, healing faster, living longer, and so
forth? Another difference is that the baby bakes faster, six
months for full werewolves, and seven for humans. Also,
you'll go into heat, like you are now. As much as I'm dying
to have you, I don't want you angry with me if you don't

want to have children now."

Moving her head, she kissed his hand as she said, "I never thought I would be lucky enough to have a man like you to have children with."

She started moving up and down his dick again, moaning. Kirby bit his hand, and he had to count to fifty with his eyes shut. She was gorgeous, her head was thrown back, her back arched, and her breasts pointed toward him in offering as she moved up and down.

When he opened his eyes it was to lust filled brown ones staring at him, and her mouth hovered over him as she purred, "Mmm, I want to have your children. I would be honored to have a child with you. Do you want to have a child now, Rane, or do you want to wait? I...ah, oh, ah."

He roared with joy and happiness. She leaned forward to his shoulder and bit so hard he knew she drew blood. She writhed on top of him, coming around his cock.

He flipped her over so she was on all fours. She fought back for the dominant place. He spread her legs as far apart as they would go and smacked her curvaceous, round bottom. Then he leaned down and licked her from clit to pussy, lapping up her juices. "Ah, little red, you taste even better than you smell."

She mewled and pushed her pussy back against his

face, demanding more. "Suck me harder, Rane. Come on, I need... Oh, just fuck me, fuck me."

Rane smacked her arse again and growled against her pussy. "No moving."

She shivered as he added a finger to her pussy whilst he sucked her clit. Kirby screamed her orgasm out as he added another finger and gave her clit a gentle nip.

Moving up her body, Rane blanketed her back, which held her more securely in place. He positioned his dick at her pussy opening and slammed home. She screamed out his name chanting, "Oh, yes! More, harder, Raannee."

He moved one of his hands around and played with her plump, jiggling breast. Shutting his eyes, he concentrated on the feel of her satin smooth skin and moved his other hand so he could explore her perfect, lush body. Her back arched. She shivered and writhed, pushing her body back against him.

He moved one hand back to support her, and she picked her pace up, pushing back on his dick, yelling, "I need to come. Rane, harder, make me come."

Kirby taunted him, and started fighting again for dominance. So she'd had enough of Mr. Nice, Gentle Guy. He growled and gave her what she wanted, pulling almost all the way out, then launching into her at the same time as he bit down on her shoulder to hold her in place.

She screamed in pleasure. "Yes, yes, that's it, I'm going to... Oh, Rane, I'm going to... Rane."

Her pussy muscles squeezed the life out of his cock. He pinched her clit and gently stroked it whilst she came. He roared his own release as he slammed home twice more. She bit his hand when the base of his dick swelled.

He moved them to the side to snuggle, and she rested her head against his chest and mumbled, "I love my werewolf."

He froze, wishing he could see her face. Scared that he had imagined it, hoping this time she said it she wasn't in heat and meant it. He wrapped his arms tighter around her, debating whether he should ask her if she meant it.

Sighing, he leaned down and kissed her neck, whispering, "You okay, little red?"

"Mmm, soooo good. Give me a couple of minutes and I'll be ready to go again."

He chuckled and kissed her neck again. Noticing her breathing had slowed, he moved himself so he could get a better look at her face, only to see she was fast asleep.

Chapter 12

By five PM Kirby was out of heat, and Rane knew that she was pregnant. He tried not to think of that as they drove to the military base. She sat beside him because she wanted to come along and practice controlling her animal element. He glanced at her. The only reason he said yes was because she'd promised not to overdo it. It had also helped that with her being with him he could keep a better eye on her. He really did have to do some work and he had to check on her brothers.

He frowned as they walked into a too quiet military base. Rane pulled his phone out only to swear as he saw he had missed three messages. Putting the phone up to his ear, he listened.

Message one: "Rane, you have become a pussy. The training course you have here is for children. There is nothing hard about it. I have taken all of the men out for a challenge, so when you stop getting your dick tickled come find us on the beach."

"Fuck, Cullen."

The second message was from Faith. She wanted to be the first to congratulate them.

The third message was from Jamie: "Rane, get your arse down here before Cullen kills all of the humans. Look, I will take over for you, I do like redheads."

Rane growled, thinking of many ways to smash Jamie into a thousand pieces. He turned to Kirby and said, "Little red, we need to get to the beach now."

She smiled at him, moving her hand up his chest.

He grabbed it and kissed it. "I really wish we were going to the beach for something nice." He pulled her along and continued. "Come on, a werewolf named Major Cullen needs to take a break."

She frowned but followed him.

* * * *

Kirby couldn't believe what she saw when she walked down the beach. Eleven men were in full gear with huge backpacks on. They were jumping off the highest cliff into the water then swimming back, repeating the process again and again. Her brother Hayden was one of the jumpers. Another six men were buried, and all that she could see were their heads as the wave receded. A large man, werewolf she felt, was kicking sand in their faces and yelling at them. Kirby continued to watch as waves crashed over their heads, keeping them submerged until the waves receded again, and again. Kirby saw red and ran toward the large werewolf. Rane tried to grab her but she was so furious she glared at him straight in the eyes and said, "Stay, freeze."

His eyes went wide as he froze in the spot. She turned and went straight to the large man. He was once again kicking sand in her brother Logan's face. This, she assumed, must be Major Cullen. He kicked sand in the next man's face and he coughed. As she got closer she could see Devlin standing by the water as the five other men continued to jump off the cliff and swim. When he saw her, he started walking over to her. She arrived at Major Cullen only to see two of the men had blue lips and were as white as ghosts. They almost looked dead. Before he could move back to her brother again she spoke up.

"If you don't stop now you will seriously regret it." She stood with her hands on her hips and glared.

He glanced her way and smiled. "What will you do, woman? Human woman, I might add. Go back home."

He shooed her away, but not before she saw her brother wince, which made Major Cullen grin. She grinned too because she was pissed now.

"I really wouldn't do that if I were you." She knew she had a wicked grin on her face.

He turned fully now and looked her over. "Are you

going to stop me?"

He smiled and she heard Rane growl, still in the stop she had told him to stay.

Devlin came to her. "Kirby, let's go. Rane will sort this out."

Jamie came from somewhere behind her and tried to guide her, which just made her angrier. Her brother seemed to smother a chuckle as she stomped her foot.

"Take your hands off me now, Jamie."

He took them away and Devlin froze, looking at her. She shivered in disgust as Major Cullen grinned and reached to touch her, the growling from Rane was extremely loud.

"Call them in," she ordered.

Major Cullen shook his head and frowned as he called a halt to the five men jumping from the cliff, and called them over, then he turned to her. "So, little redhead, do you have a name?"

She continued grinning. "It's Kirby Brown."

Rane roared in frustration. "Wolfen."

She shrugged. "Wolfen now, I suppose."

Jamie laughed and Devlin chuckled, and the major's eyes grew wider.

"Are you related to this Brown?" He kicked sand at

Logan, and this got her more pissed off. No more Miss Nice Girl.

She jumped up at him, smacking his nose, and said, "Bad, bad dog. Down now on all fours, no changing."

He froze and did as she said. She glanced behind her to see Jamie and Devlin doubled over laughing. The major stared up at her from all fours, his eyes wide as he muttered, "How on earth... Magic doesn't work on werewolves."

She laughed. "You haven't heard the good news. Fate has changed the game a little bit. You see, because I am a mate and have some werewolf magic, my powers now work on werewolves too." She looked down at him and giggled. "Isn't that great?"

The major's eyes widened even more.

She continued to smile down at him as she shouted, "Rane, you can come now. The bad dog is not going anywhere, are you?"

Her brothers and the other men were smothering chuckles.

Rane's arms came around her as he said against her neck, "Don't do something so foolish again. I need to protect you. It's not just you now, you have to be more careful, you're pregnant."

He turned her in his arms and kissed her lips. She

heard her brothers choking; Logan was swearing and trying to get out of the sand. When she turned and saw the state her brothers were in she smacked the major again.

"How long have they been doing this?" She smacked him again as he tried to get up to answer. "Stay, you don't move until I say so. How long?" She was so angry she said this in all the wolves' heads, and they winced.

Major Cullen muttered, "Since six this morning."

"What! You have to be joking. No wonder they look almost dead." She whacked him again.

Rane growled as he said, "We need them tomorrow."

"Do you need the major tonight?" Kirby asked.

Rane sighed, but they were shocked as Kane spoke up as he came over with Faith following behind. "Cullen, they look like corpses." Kane turned to Kirby. "Did you do this to him? Because he isn't standing to greet his alpha."

Kirby shrugged. "He's an arsehole. I'm teaching him a lesson."

Faith laughed and clapped her hands. "All we have to do is get you mad. Look at you."

Rane groaned and hugged her tighter.

Jamie laughed. "You should have seen her, she even froze Rane. It was hilarious. She told Cullen that he was a bad dog and whacked him on the nose."

Faith giggled and Kane turned and raised an eyebrow at her. Kirby shrugged again and then turned back to Cullen.

"Okay, up now. Let's go, I'm going to have to check all of the men over," said Kane.

Cullen didn't move, he just glared at Kirby. Kane went to help him and Kirby was still so frigging angry as she glared at Kane. "Don't move him, don't touch him."

Kane froze halfway leaning down. Faith's giggle turned into laughter, Jamie and Devlin joined in, and even Rane chuckled. Kane glared at her, which she swore a weaker man or woman would've caved at.

"Release me now."

Kirby shivered at the power of that order. "I'll let you up if you promise you won't touch the major, he will not be moving. I really hope you don't need him tonight."

Kane sighed and looked behind her at Rane which just pissed her off more.

"Kirby, he was just doing his job."

She raised her eyebrow at Kane. "So his job is to kill these men before the demons and minions do?"

Kane winced and sighed again. "Okay, I promise not to touch him."

She let him go, and he straightened and looked at Rane.

"I think we need to bring Cullen in our van tomorrow, so she can be angry when we go into the tunnels."

Rane chuckled and kissed her forehead, and his chuckle turned into a growl. "I don't want her to come, because it's too dangerous."

She frowned and looked up at Rane. "Don't even think about me not coming tomorrow." She looked at Kane again. "If Cullen does what these guys did here until morning will he still be able to come tomorrow?"

Kane grinned. "Piece of cake, as long as he gets at least three or four hours sleep."

She groaned and looked at Rane. "I don't want it to be a piece of cake. What will make it hard?"

Rane kissed her lips, chuckling against them. "Little red, we are werewolves, what these boys—I mean men— did today is what we do to start our training at seventeen or eighteen."

She gasped and her hand went straight to her stomach. She didn't even realize she'd done that until she glanced down.

Faith chuckled. She went over to Cullen, who was still on all fours, and placed her hands on him. She swore and said one word, "Powerful" before she fell.

Kirby shook herself as she snapped Cullen out of his

command, yelling at him to grab Faith. Seconds later, Kane grabbed her off a terrified Cullen, yelling at everyone behind him to follow now. They walked up the winding path for a few minutes until Kirby saw Kane's house coming into view. When they reached the large back doors Kane turned with Faith still in his arms.

"Rane, take them all into the lounge room. Take the ones that are still blue and warm them slowly." He smiled down at her. "Call my parents and tell them to get over here. Could you please check on Remy? I think even Ben is getting sick of her surliness. If she hears all of the noise she'll want to know what's going on. I cannot wait until Arden gets here."

Half an hour later Faith came to, to a strained room anxiously waiting for the information on the vision. Glancing around, she looked right at Cullen but spoke to Kirby.

"No punishing him, Kirby. Tomorrow will be enough punishment. We need to leave tonight and be ready to hit the demon stronghold at first light." Tears were streaming down Faith's face as she looked at Cullen. "You need to be one of the first in, Cullen, and go down the tunnels to the right as far as you can. Keep going right, follow your nose before you open a door, and make sure you are not in half-change mode." Faith started to sob. "I don't…I don't know how long she has been down there, she…she… Oh, she's so young. I don't even know if she's as old as me." She paused and looked Cullen straight in his eyes. "No growling, don't growl at her."

Cullen was pale and was growling, his hands had changed and his fists were clenched.

Faith sobbed again. "We need to go now. We need to go now, please. I know they have thirty-six people down there. Most of them are women. Eight of them… Oh God, eight of those…" She buried her face in Kane's chest. "Eight of those are children."

Kirby could feel tears falling down her own face.

Faith then looked around the whole room. "We're going to need everyone, and I mean everyone." She looked at Jack. "I mean all the women fighters, even elders capable of leading. You're going to need someone strong to hand things over to, because you're going to have to fight too, Jack. It's a pity Arden won't arrive until tomorrow afternoon. The poor new werewolves won't even get to have one peaceful night in a bed before they fight."

Faith sighed and looked at her. "Kirby, you will have to be like you were today, we're going to need you. You have to rest now, because tomorrow is going to be a big day. We are going to win. We are going to save them all, because we have to." She snuggled into Kane and fell into an exhausted sleep.

Chapter 13

Rane carried his sleeping mate to the van. The doors opened and he could see everyone had already been picked up. There was Cullen, Jamie, Devlin, Griffen, Logan, his granddad, Sandra, and Kane, who also had his mate in his arms, Faith. It was one full minibus. His dad was driving, and his mum sat in the passenger seat. Logan looked extremely uncomfortable. When he saw Rane with Kirby in his arms, he had a worried look on his face.

Rane wondered what his sisters were up to and who was looking after them as his grandmother was directing and organizing people so new houses and rooms would be ready for the survivors. "Who's looking after the girls?"

His mum turned to face him in her seat. "Ava decided to stay back. All the women that are left are pitching in, helping to have everything ready for worst case scenario and best."

Rane nodded, knowing it was the best plan. His sister Ava had never been a fighter like her twin Eve. Ava was the mothering type, and very bossy. She was always cooking, cleaning, looking after children, and pretty much trying to organize everyone.

Turning to Kane he asked, "What time will we get there? It's late now and when I spoke to you earlier, you said the ten enforcer groups that were still out patrolling would meet us there."

"It'll take about three and half hours to get to our destination, and set up will take twenty to thirty minutes. I'm hoping to sleep now, so I'm more than ready for what's to come."

Rane grimaced and hugged Kirby tighter to him before he rested his eyes and drifted to sleep.

Rane woke as the van stopped. He looked around to see hills and grass land—a farming community. *A good place to hide*, he thought. Rane saw that already three large tents had been put up and everyone around was hauling equipment. He got out, careful not to wake Kirby as he walked over toward six military trucks and two medical military tents. A very determined, tall black man stalked toward them, his eyebrows drawn together and his jaw locked, like he was grinding his teeth. His fists were clenched at his sides.

He turned to Kane. "I know they've brought doctors, but who's that guy headed straight for us, because I know he's not military."

Kane kissed Faith's head and hugged her tighter as he

answered. "Faith said we should bring him. She thought we would need him. Jerome Stark is a friend of mine from the hospital I used to work at. He's the doctor that operated on Faith." Kane put up his hand awkwardly around Faith. "I know, I know before you say it, Faith said she had a feeling...well, she really said there won't be enough doctors or medical staff, and I needed to get the military to give us more medical people and call in a friend. She then suggested Jerome. She also said that he would keep our secret and that he would come in handy in the future."

Rane grinned at his brother as he continued.

"She wants him for her baby doctor." Rane chuckled as Kane growled out. "She said I would not be able to deliver our baby, and since she isn't allowed to go to a normal doctor she wanted the next best thing."

Faith moaned, waking up in Kane's arms. "You've got that right," she said. "There's no way my mate is watching down there while I squeeze a werewolf baby out. If your mother goes on one more time about how she did it all by herself with you guys, I swear I'll knock her out."

Rane bit his lip, trying not to laugh so he didn't wake up Kirby, but the look on Faith's face... He gave in and gave a big belly laugh just as Dr. Jerome Stark came upon them.

"What the hell is going on, Kane?"

Kane sighed and Faith jumped out of Kane's arms, straightened, and looked Jerome in the eye. "You're not going to believe us unless you're shown. Kane, change to full wolf and give him fifteen minutes to get used to it before you change to half-change. Then we'll tell him what we can ...if he doesn't pass out," she added.

Kane changed into a big, dirty blond wolf and to Jerome's credit he only stepped back two paces, rubbed his eyes, and looked around him, then looked at Faith.

Rane could feel Kirby waking up. She stretched and kissed him on the cheek before getting down.

Faith was explaining as much as possible to Jerome, and he was doing fine until Kane changed into half-change werewolf mode. Jerome yelled, "Holy shit. You're a monster." He darted glances around them and slowly walked away mumbling, "Crap! I didn't sign up for this shit. What the hell is this world coming to?"

Rane walked with Kirby in silence to the largest tent where everyone was. There were one hundred and twenty-six werewolves, including women and other weres, eleven trained military men, eight human mates with powers ranging from water elements, earth elements, air elements, witches, and of course an animal affinity, and psychic.

Rane shut his eyes, hoping there were a lot less demons then they originally thought because all up they only numbered one hundred and forty-five. They had even brought two away teams home and had new werewolves sent over from overseas. The problem was they were a small pack to begin with, and the land mass they protected was so large.

Rane walked over to his dad who was standing with Tray, Cullen, his mother, and Blake.

"How's it all going, Dad?"

His dad let out a weary sigh. "How do you think, son? I have two werewolves coming out of retirement, and five elders helping with communications. On the positive side, Arden will be coming here instead of home, he'll be here any minute, and Eve was granted leave and will be arriving in about fifteen minutes, so that will be an extra two. Oh, and Lexie is an earth element, she has been communicating with the earth. Here is the worst news of all—the tunnels are everywhere in this region. At the moment she's with the elders helping map as much as she can. The witches are doing good though—they're coming up with a spell to cloak us so we don't draw attention when we bring out the injured and any rescued supernaturals. Last, but certainly not least, Sara is with a conjurer, and they're at the well, using the water to ice extra blades and knives."

Kane nodded to his dad, and Kirby spoke up with a question he should have thought to ask. "Can Lexie feel where the rooms are, or where the tunnels are bigger?"

His father smiled at Kirby. "I thought Rane would've asked that question." His dad winked at him. "That's probably the best news so far...she's found fifteen rooms, one that she said was bigger than the rest. We think that's the one that will have the most demons and minions. Sorry, Kirby, but that's where we're going to need your help."

Rane couldn't contain the growl and he snapped at his dad. "No fucking way is my mate going to be going into a room where you think the most demons will be. Not going to happen. I don't want her here in the first place, because she's not experienced enough." He held up his hand before his dad had a chance to butt in. "I know you didn't let Mum do any fighting. I know she did do some a time or two but by then she'd had forty to fifty years of training. Whereas Kirby was thrown in five days ago, so fuck no. It's bad enough she'll be down there at all, but there's no way she's going into that big room."

He had growled out the last bit so loud that everyone was now looking at them. An elbow to his stomach made him look down into furious brown eyes and a face set in an angry frown. Kirby's cheeks were bright red and her hands were on her hips.

"Do you want me to show you how good I have become, again?" she said through clenched teeth. He went to put his hands around her, when she yelled, "Change now."

He and all the werewolves in the room changed

She looked down at him in wolf form. "How's that?"

She walked toward the exit only to be stopped by Arden, as he looked around the room, then at Kirby. "Holy shit! Faith and Rane weren't kidding."

Eve came in beside Arden and burst out laughing. He watched in wolf form as Eve pulled Kirby in for a hug, saying, "I'm going to love you. You are so perfect for Rane. Welcome to the family."

* * * *

Kirby stood at one of the five entrances they had made for the tunnels. Rane was behind her, still furious. Jack and Della were in front of her, Logan was on one side, Faith on the other with Kane, Cullen, David, and forty-five other werewolves, and her youngest brother Hayden was at the back.

She took one last deep breath as they walked into the start of the tunnels. They were the group heading to the large room with eight rooms off it. Lexie had told them that they would walk down for about ten to fifteen minutes without coming onto anything else, and then three tunnels would come into view. They were told to go straight if they were going to the large room. Ten werewolves broke off, five for each of the other tunnels.

Jack kicked down the door and before her were easily over one hundred demons of all shapes and sizes. The thing that had her even more terrified was there were over one thousand, she thought, minions. The minions charged them, and Kirby prayed that Logan and everyone could kill a lot before they got to her.

She yelled, using everything she had. "Stop, freeze."

The minions closest to them froze, which gave the werewolves a chance to move forward, killing as many as they could to get to the demons, who were now joining the werewolves.

The second wave of minions came and Kirby screamed again and again repeating, "Stop, freeze, stop." She didn't even stop as she put her hands to her head as it started to ache. It got harder to concentrate on freezing the minions and not the werewolves.

Kirby then heard the command that had her fighting for her life. A large demon yelled, "Kill the small redhead, kill her, kill her."

Eight smaller demons came for her. Rane and Faith swore. Logan grabbed her hand, and she felt a jolt as he started yelling with her. "Stop, freeze. Stop, freeze."

Her headache eased and it became easier to focus, especially when she felt Hayden grab her other hand and join in the yelling, and almost all the minions froze. The demons roared as the minions were now easy pickings. More demons came after her, and Rane yelled at her brothers not to let go of her hands until all of the demons were dead and to guard Kirby with their lives.

Kane, David, and Rane stepped in front of them as the first eight demons attacked. Zombies came up behind them and grabbed her as a demon came at her. Hayden jumped in front of her only to get a horn in his shoulder. She screamed, lifting her long blades and bringing them down, trying not to cringe at the sound of her slicing the horn off.

Hayden amazingly kept going, even using the arm that had the horn sticking out of it. Logan was killing zombies, and Hayden was fighting with the demon. She knew Rane was going to be pissed already, so she might as well help. Feeling the demon tail come around her waist, she screamed as she chopped the tail off, and another scratched her face.

Kirby knew from watching Faith the head had to be cut

Rane's Mate / Hazel Gower

off, and their heart had to be pulled out and stabbed with the
ice knife. With another yell for courage, she climbed the
demon's back, which wasn't easy as another demon was
trying to rip her off. The demon got distracted by a furious
Rane, and slowly she reached his shoulders, and without
thinking it through, she cut the head off.

Blood was everywhere, it hurt her fingers and anything
not covered. She thanked Faith for the leather outfit and the
cut off finger gloves. Falling to the floor, sharp claws
grabbed her by the throat as another tail came around to
slash her legs. As she flailed and struggled to get away, the
demon tried to reach for her knife, but his hand was
chopped off by the scariest sight she had ever seen. Rane
was roaring, flipping, spinning, slashing, and got the heart
of the demon, which caused the demon to drop her.

She crawled slowly, and stood only to be pulled the
rest of the way by her hair as a smaller demon threw her
against the wall. Getting up, she slipped in blood and kicked
a dead minion. Looking up, she saw a small seven and a
half foot demon, the smallest she had ever seen. She gripped
the long knife tighter, and the demon grinned, showing
long, sharp teeth. Kirby took a hesitant step forward just as
it lunged. She dodged and screamed as the horn ripped
down her arm. The demon's head came up and his hand

Page 205

came out, she screamed as she cut it off and tripped over a dead demon. The demon she was fighting laughed then wrapped his tail around her waist, pulling her up. She clenched her teeth, determined not to scream again and satisfy him with her pain. Using what strength she had, she chopped off the tail around her waist and backed into a wolf fighting.

The werewolf turned and placed another knife in her hand and then ran for a demon's head. The small demon was still stalking her and she chanced a quick look around for help, but everyone was fighting a demon.

Faith and Kane had three circling them. Rane and her brothers had five and they weren't doing so good. Jack and Della were currently surrounded by eight demons.

She groaned, straightening her shoulders and telling herself to suck it up because she had to help the others. She could do this. She took another glance around then roared, attacking the small demon, slashing and twirling. Her height actually came in handy as she could sneak under things. She jumped on his body and stabbed his chest, moving the knife around until she found his heart. He clawed at her back until she heard the pop, then his heart froze, and she shattered it into a million pieces.

Two minions came out of a room, and she ordered

them to "Kill demons, kill demons, take off their heads. Help me take off their heads."

They attacked the demons. Kirby could hear the demons were trying to change her orders, but it was too late. She finished the demon and turned to help the wolf who had given her the new knife. She then turned her focus on Rane and her brothers. Hayden was barely standing, and both Rane and Logan were covered in blood and cuts.

Kirby ran, jumping over bodies, and continued to tell the minions to kill the demons. She pointed to the ones she wanted, ordering them to "Kill them, get their heads, kill them."

Kirby reached her brothers just as Hayden fell to the floor. She screamed as the demon was about the rip Hayden's head off. Kirby barreled onto Hayden, and he helped her gain her balance as she was slashed across the back by the demon's sharp claws. Rane heard her scream, which only seemed to make him angrier and give him a second wind.

Kirby ran under hands and climbed up the front of the demon while two minions were being killed. She stabbed the demon's heart as his tail stabbed her in the leg. It was still embedded as she turned, but Hayden cut if off. Hayden was white and barely alive.

Rane's Mate / Hazel Gower

Calling to any leftover minions, Kirby told them, "Come now, kill the demons."

Six flew in and went straight for the demons surrounding her.

She repeated her orders again and again. "Chop off their heads, kill them."

Kirby went for one of the two demons going for Logan, who didn't look in much better condition than Hayden. She turned as a werewolf woman came in the door with fifteen other werewolves and roared. The female werewolf went straight to Hayden, finishing off the demon that was about to pick Hayden up.

Kirby was so shocked she lost her concentration and the minions changed directions, going for them again. She shook her head as Logan of all people yelled, "Focus, Kirby, focus."

She turned back and chanted, "Kill the demons, go for their heads."

Running for her brother, she swerved around one demon's tail, chopping it off as it tried to wrap around her leg. Another demon's tail came around her arm, embedding into her. She moaned as she cut it off, pulling the arrow head out and climbing on the closest demon's back, all the time still chanting to the minions.

Kirby knew she was tiring because she started to feel the demons' thoughts through the mind link she had with the minions. The demons were whispering in her head, telling her to kill the werewolves and other nasty things that they wanted to do to her.

Finally reaching the top of the demon's back, she hugged his neck and pulled the knife toward her, screaming as she fell to the floor. Crawling over to the other demon, she went through the whole process again of climbing up his back. She was exhausted and it was slippery now as blood covered her body. Kirby slipped and was dangling off the demon's back. Rane roared as he came up to her, which helped give her renewed strength, and she climbed the last bit up, wrapping her arms around his neck and pulling her arms with the knives in them toward her.

Kirby fell to the floor onto the dead bodies of thousands of minions and demons. She crawled over to Logan who was now leaning against the wall. No, it wasn't a wall, it was a door. Her brother groaned and slowly, together, they opened it and stared in shock at a small room where four children were huddled together, hiding in the furthest corner—two boys and two girls, ranging she guessed from the ages of three to eight. Four bowls sat on the opposite side of the room that smelled of feces and urine. Kirby choked on a sob as she took a deep breath, stood up straight, which was extremely painful, and dropped the knives that were in her hands.

Kirby held her hands up in the universal sign of surrender. She knew her voice was rough from yelling and she must look like feral. Sighing in relief as a big, beautiful tree bark wolf who she knew was Rane came up next to her, she rested her hand on him, using him to hold her up, as she said, "Hi there. I won't hurt you, I promise. All of the monsters are dead, they're gone now. They can't hurt you again. My name is Kirby. My friends and I came here to help you. We're going to take you somewhere safe where there is plenty of water and food." One of the kids perked up so she continued on. "There is sunshine up there. I'm going to take you out of here. I promise I won't hurt you."

The oldest of the group who seemed to be the leader spoke up very quietly. "What's that with you? It is really big."

She forced a smile. "What do you think it is?"

The little boy looked at Rane and took a hesitant step forward. "It looks like a really big dog. I haven't seen a big dog in a long time because I've been down here a long time."

Kirby knew that there were tears rolling down her face

as she asked, "Would you like to come with me and get out of here?"

The boy looked behind himself at the other children, then he turned back and took a really good look at her. He seemed to concentrate as he asked, "Will you hurt us?"

Kirby forced another smile. "No. I'm here to save you."

The boy looked back at the three other kids, nodded, and then turned back to Kirby. He raised an eyebrow as he asked, "Are they dogs that you brought?"

Kirby thought about the answer, because something didn't feel right. Out of all the questions she thought he might ask that wasn't one of them. Knowing she needed to tread carefully to gain the children's trust, she said, "They are very special, and they would never hurt you."

The boy took a small step forward. "You're telling the truth. What are they?"

She frowned at the odd phrasing. "Well, they're special. What would you do if I told you Rane here is a wolf?"

The little boy's eyes widened, and one of the children gasped. The little boy who was speaking smiled. "Is he a friendly wolf?" The boy looked behind her. "You have lots of them."

Kirby slowly turned to see red, gray, dark brown, white, and brown wolves. Della also stood with Eve and a few other people that she didn't know. She turned back to the children. "All these people came to help save everyone down here and bring you all to the surface so you can see the sun and the water."

The little boy went over to the three other children and picked up the youngest boy, who couldn't have been more than three. He was a tiny thing. "Come on, she was telling the truth the whole time."

Kirby mentally kicked herself. She should have realized that he was a truth detector. The four children slowly walked toward her. Her brother Logan took a step toward them, but she put her arm out to stop him and said, "They need to come by themselves, it would help build trust."

The little boy turned to her and pointed to the oldest girl who she guessed to be around seven. "This is Renee." He then moved down to the little girl holding Renee's hand. "This here is Brat."

Kirby gasped, looking at the boy as she said, "Did I just hear you right? What did you call her?"

"Brat, that's what they called her, and she was too little to know her name when they brought her in here."

Kirby shook her head as tears rolled down her cheeks. Della came in and got down to eye level with the little girl that they called Brat. Tears were rolling down Della's cheeks as she said, "Hi, sweetheart. Would you like us to give you a new name?"

The little girl nodded hesitantly, and Della continued, "I think you look like a Miss Molly, so how about Molly?"

The little girl smiled, and Della said, "Hi, Molly. My name is Della, and Kirby here has introduced herself, but that man over there is Logan, and lastly, as you heard her say, that wolf is Rane. Come on, there are lots out there that are just like Rane to meet."

Della held her hands out, and Renee and Molly hesitantly took them. They walked out of the room trailing Della. The little boy that Kirby had been talking to turned to her.

"Hi, Kirby. My name is Mick, and this here is Useless, well that's what they called him, but I called him Blue, 'cause his eyes remind me of the sky, I remember that."

Kirby smiled at Mick. "I like that, how about we stick with Blue? I like it a lot better than the other name."

The boys nodded. "Are we really going outside?"

"Yes. There will be a lot of people, and more wolves. They're all friendly, and they're here to help. Are you ready to come out now?"

He nodded and they followed Della out of the tunnel slowly. As they reached the top, the boys gripped her hands tighter, and she could see tears rolling down Mick's face. She turned to face him. "It's okay to be scared. If you want I could lift you and Blue and carry you out." She was exhausted but she knew she could muster the strength, especially if he needed the comfort. Mick looked her up and down, and Kirby straightened the best she could. "I'm a lot stronger than I look."

He didn't say anything just moved closer and stood in front of her and nodded. She picked Mick up, placing him on one hip, and then she picked up Blue, placing him on the other. "When we go outside the sun will be bright, so if you don't want to hurt your eyes bury your face in my shoulder."

They both nodded, burying their faces when the door opened and she walked out into the mid-day sun.

Chapter 14

They had set up six extra-large tents, and people were running everywhere. It looked like controlled chaos. Three of the large tents were medical stations. The other tents were military central.

The boys clung to Kirby, but every now and then they would peek out from being buried in her shoulder. Kirby continued to follow Della who went to a large, open, airy tent where several other werewolves and lost scared people stood, taking everything in. Della moved to a corner with four chairs and sat with the youngest girl on her lap. Kirby followed, sitting slowly with her precious cargo. Looking up, she noticed Rane nod to his mother then take off.

"Are doctors going to come and check the children out, or are we going to wait until they are comfortable and at home?"

Della smiled at her and nodded to the boys who were now sitting up and looking around with smiles on their faces. "I think it's best if we get them home first and have the doctors check them there. Let them enjoy their freedom for now."

"We really are saved," Mick said. A few tears were

rolling down his face.

Blue was jumping up and down on her, and an involuntary wince escaped her. Blue hesitantly got down, still gripping her arm as he tried to spin in circles. Mick joined him. The sun shone bright, and the boys and girls went just outside the tent opening. Tears were rolling down Kirby's face, and she sighed in relief as familiar muscular arms came around her. Rane leaned down and kissed her forehead.

"Little red, you did good. Look at them enjoying their freedom. You helped give them that. I'm so proud of you. I'm sorry I tried to hold you back, not wanting you to fight. I should have had more faith in you. You were amazing, and I don't know how we would have done it without you."

She stood up and turned in his arms, nodding to Della who walked over to stand by the children who were now dancing in the sunlight. She smiled up at him.

"You're forgiven. This whole experience has opened my eyes in so many ways. It has made me relook and think about the goals that I have. You were right, I wasn't prepared but…" She reached up and touched his lips to stop him from talking. "If it wasn't for me jumping into this situation, I don't know if I would know my potential for my gift. I definitely know my confidence wouldn't have had this huge increase. I love the fact that I helped save all of these people, and, Rane, you were fantastic in action."

He kissed her gently on the lips as he whispered, "You did good, little red, you can let go now. Let it all go."

As soon as he said that Kirby took a deep breath and collapsed into his arms, her adrenaline finally running out. Rane picked her up and sat on the edge of a chair, turning her so she could see Della and the children.

"How come your mum is still going? She barely has a bruise."

Rane hugged her tighter. "Werewolf genes. She'll be completely healed by tonight."

Kirby groaned and snuggled closer, wincing as her own bruises and cuts made themself known. She fought to stay awake as she watched the children. Looking around again, she stood up, yelping in pain, and said, "Where are my brothers? They were behind me I'm sure."

She tried to get further out of Rane's arms, but he pulled her back down and held her tighter. He kissed both of her cheeks, and then her lips again gently before he said, "They are both in medical being seen by a doctor. I checked on them quickly before I came back to you, they'll be fine. They'll be sore though, although Hayden will feel better a lot sooner than Logan, thanks to Sandra." He kissed her lips again. "We will have an extra person this weekend, Sandra mated Hayden."

Kirby chuckled. "I thought it was strange when that woman went crazy to protect Hayden. Poor Sandra."

Kane chuckled. "More like poor Hayden, because Sandra has been dying for a mate. She won't take any bullshit. Sorry, sweetheart, you do realize that he will now have all the advantages that you have."

Kirby groaned. "I was so looking forward to getting a chance at finally beating them in something."

He chuckled again and hugged her tighter. They sat for another fifteen minutes in silence, just enjoying watching as another four children joined the others in dancing.

"What's going to happen now, Rane?"

He sighed. "I should be talking to the military leader and working, not sitting here with you. It's just when I'm with you, you make me take a breather and enjoy life, take it all in. For once in my life I'm not career minded."

Kirby couldn't help herself, she reached up and pulled his face down to hers, kissing him slowly, tracing his lips until they opened and his tongue met hers. They pulled away as eight different 'yucks' and giggles were heard.

* * * *

Rane smiled as a blushing Kirby turned to the crowd.

He was the luckiest man to have her for his mate, she was everything and more than what he expected—she was his perfect match. He knew he had fallen madly in love with her. He wondered if she knew the power she had over him.

Rane had never felt this good in his life, even with his cracked ribs, broken arm, bruised and cut up. The children were asking Kirby about her special powers as they were telling theirs. He chuckled as she called to Duncan and Tristan who came over very reluctantly, not looking too happy, but as soon as they saw the children they gave their full cooperation, and he felt Kirby sigh in his arms. She got them to do all sorts of things to amuse the children.

His mother wandered off for a while, then came back to take the kids to their new homes. Rane could see the children were exhausted from all the excitement, and he knew Kirby wasn't doing much better. She was now leaning right back on him, and he could tell she wasn't using her powers on Duncan and Tristan; they were now doing things to amuse the kids seeing the state she was in.

His mother whispered, "We're going to move out, there will still be clean up and we're going to do something about closing and destroying all the tunnels. Arden, Devlin, Jamie, and Griffen are going to sort out the military so you can stay with Kirby. We're going to settle the eight children at my house, Ava is there and I have your younger sisters to help. I also think Grace and Sophie will love to help too. I've spoken to some elders who are eager to help, they've even asked to adopt some of the children, which is positive news. Let's get home, as everyone is exhausted. Kane hasn't left Faith's side, carrying her everywhere, and Tray is no better. You should be so proud of Kirby. She was amazing."

He smiled and stood with Kirby in his arms. "Thanks, Mum. Let's get into the van."

Chapter 15

They arrived home to the sun setting over the water. Kirby had insisted on staying at his parents' house to help out with the children. When they had finally got in bed, she had snuggled into him and he'd tried to kiss her and feel her up. Kirby had swatted him, turning bright red as she stated, "We're at your parents' house, so no funny business."

He lay there and watched her sleep, thinking of the miracle she was to him. He finally drifted to sleep with his hand over her stomach where their child grew.

Early the next morning he woke to loud children's laughter, music, singing, and yelling. He smiled as Kirby snuggled into him. "No, just give me ten more minutes. I will be good, I promise."

Rane chuckled. "Really, little red? How good?"

He pressed his rock hard erection between the cheeks of her arse, and she moaned, wiggling her arse, nestling his cock were she wanted it. He growled and nipped her ear and moved down her neck. Kirby arched into him, moaning. "I love waking up in the morning now. There is always someone happy to see me."

He laughed and turned her to face him so he could

show her just how happy he was. Fastening his mouth over hers, his hands slowly moved up her taut stomach to his favorite play things. He gently pulled on one pointed nipple, and she moaned and moved as close as she could get, rubbing herself on him.

They groaned together as they heard his mother call through the door. "Rane! The general has been calling, I think you should call him back before we're invaded by the military. Oh, and Kirby, sweetheart, your brothers called. You should call them, they sounded pretty desperate."

Rane sighed and kissed Kirby again before he answered his mother. "Okay, we're up. We will be ten minutes."

His mother chuckled. "Just remember you're in a full house, with children."

Kirby buried her face in his shoulder. "I'm so embarrassed, you've turned me into a sex maniac."

He got out of bed, laughing, pulling her with him. An hour later they were downstairs and Rane was calling Arden, Griffen, and Devlin. He needed to meet and to talk to them. Rane knew now that he had a mate he wouldn't be able to keep up with his grueling work schedule. He had loved working eighteen hour days, but now he loved something more, and he wanted to have time with her. Rane was going to do something he had never done before—ask for help, giving up work duties. He knew after last night with Cullen finding his mate and the state she was in, Cullen would be cutting his hours back too.

Rane met Griffen, Devlin, and Arden—who looked like shit—in Faith's special place in the woods. Rane cleared his throat, hating the thought that his brothers would have to get more involved. He shut his eyes, and Kirby's fire engine hair and her smiling face, along with her big brown eyes, flashed before him. He smiled as he opened his eyes, knowing he was doing the right thing. He needed to stop being a workaholic.

He was surprised to see that Cullen had joined them. Rane didn't know who looked worse, Arden or Cullen. Rane raised his eyebrow at Cullen as he said, "I don't care if he is the general, if he calls one more time, I'm going to shove the phone up his arse."

Rane smirked, because he knew from the smile on Cullen's face he was one hundred percent serious. He nodded to Cullen. "It's good you're here, because I came to discuss work. We both have mates now, we can't do the eighteen hour days anymore. I'm not saying there isn't anyone qualified enough to take over our job, I know if Devlin and Arden and all of us share the work—"

"I'll help too, and so will Jamie."

Rane swore as he turned to see his brother Kane and Jamie join them. Kane had a feral look on his face, like he had just done something. "What the fuck have you done, Kane? You're alpha, not military go-to. You didn't even join the field duty. You were in the military medical."

Kane chuckled. "That's what I let you all think. I mean it. We will all help, and I just showed the general and a couple of other heads of the human military who is really in charge."

Rane and Cullen swore. "Kane, we need to be on good footing with them."

If at all possible Kane's grin got bigger. "Oh, we are on the best footing, and what I'm about to tell you is extremely classified. I wouldn't be telling you if Faith hadn't told me that all of you need to know. The top five people in power…three of the five are werewolves and two are supernatural, and that's just in Australia. Most of the people in power in America are also werewolves or supernaturals. Every country on this continent has at least two werewolves in head power."

Wow. Rane knew they were infiltrated everywhere, but not that far. Before he had a chance to wrap his mind around everything that Kane had just told him, Devlin butted in.

"Then why the fuck have they been so pushy, giving us fifty new recruits to train, if the power is werewolves and paranormal?"

Kane sighed. "Because we still have to listen to others, and it is our job to protect humanity, but they need to at least be able to help protect themselves. Faith told me this morning that we need to grow and branch out if we're going to win this war."

All five werewolves groaned, because they knew that when Faith said stuff like that, they were in for big changes.

* * * *

Kirby stared in awe at the completed house. It was late Friday morning and she couldn't believe that she was staring at the same house. The house looked like it was months old, even the window ledges were painted. Yellow daises made a path from the carport, which was next to a double garage.

Rane's arms came around her. "This is a visitor's car park. Well, it's really parking for your parents since everyone else we know lives close enough to walk."

Kirby turned into his arms, stood on her tiptoes, and pulled his face down so she could kiss him. Smiling against her lips, he picked her up. She squealed as he grasped her arse, squeezing it.

Kirby laughed. "I love you. You are so good to me. I love all the little things you do for me. I love you."

Rane's hands froze mid squeeze, even the smile on his face froze, the only thing that moved was his eyes, they shone bright as he searched her face. He seemed to come back to himself just as she started to get scared that maybe she shouldn't have said anything, but it had just come out.

He smiled so big. "Say it again."

Kirby breathed a sigh of relief and grinned. "Say what again?"

Rane chuckled, placing his mouth over hers and taking his time as he traced her lips before sucking the bottom lip into his mouth. Rane growled when she bit his bottom lip and their tongues meet, mimicking the dance of love.

Rane moved them against the front door, then pulled her sundress over her head. His own shirt followed, falling somewhere on the ground. She couldn't undo the buttons on his jeans fast enough, and gave a sigh of relief when they were undone. His thick erection popped free. Shivering in anticipation, she moved her hand up and down his muscular chest, giving his nipples a light pinch and loving when it made him crazy. Kirby loved it when he got all dominant.

He pulled his mouth away from hers and looked into

her eyes. "Woman, you burn me, every time I touch you, I catch alight."

Rane growled, pushed her up against the door, and dived in straight for her pussy. Her head fell back against the door as he sucked on her, pulling her erect nub into his mouth, growling, which sent shivers pulsing through her body. She felt her pussy convulse and knew she was soaking wet. God, she loved his growling, it was so sexy.

He moaned against her pussy as he lapped at her juices. "Oh, Rane, please I'm going to... Oh, make me..."

Rane growled again and added a thick finger to join his tongue.

Her hand came down to grip his hair as his nipped her clit and added a second finger, which made her come undone. "Ahhh, I love that mouth of yours."

Rane smiled up at her, and she could see herself shinning against his lips. She shivered when he licked his lips then brought his fingers up, sucking them clean, groaning. "Yum, you taste so good."

She pulled him back up by the hair so she could show him just how much she appreciated him. Taking his mouth to hers, she lined her pussy up with his cock and slid down. Tracing his mouth and tasting herself on him, she rubbed her body against his.

"I love everything about you, Rane. Your body could make a Greek god jealous." She grinned. "I love that's it's all mine, you're all mine. You fit me perfectly."

She squeezed her pussy, and his forehead fell against hers, and he moaned.

She continued, wanting to make it clear how she felt for him. "I love the way you always make sure I'm happy, satisfied first, but what I love most is your love for me in everything you do." She looked into his eyes. "I love the way you treat my brothers, especially Logan. Helping me with my fighting, cooking for me, and just doing things like putting a carport and undercover walkway, so my parents can visit. These are only some of the many reasons why I love you."

He chuckled and pushed her back against the door. His hands were cupping her breasts and slowly moved to cup her face. She looked into his electric blue eyes, and they sparkled as he spoke. "I'm the luckiest man in the world to have you. Without you, I would still be empty, working eighteen hour days. You were my world from the moment I first saw you. I couldn't grasp how lucky I am, how perfect you are for me. I have never loved anyone like I love you. I will never love anyone else. I'm so proud of you, and I'll never get enough of you. You, Kirby Wolfen, are my everything."

Tears rolled down Kirby's face.

Rane kissed them away. "Little red."

He kissed her. Kirby kissed him back, feeling the best she had ever felt in her life. No more was she the pushover. She had learnt to use her powers, and she was more powerful than ever. She had also learnt to stick up for herself and to speak up against her brothers, she had even put a tough werewolf in his place. The old Kirby would never have done anything like that.

As Rane moved again, she smiled, loving her new freedom and her new confidence. Kirby arched as Rane sucked one nipple into his mouth. She reached her arms around to hold his head. "Faster, harder, Rane. Make me scream."

She felt his smile against her skin. "Your wish is my command."

Her laughter turned into a scream as he moved and bit her shoulder, his cock slamming home. Kirby screamed her orgasm as Rane roared, slamming into her and locking. He pushed her against the door as it cracked, falling open, and Kirby laughed out on a moan.

"The best thing I ever did was move."

Rane kissed her and carried her to their bedroom.

Epilogue

Logan's body still ached all over, and he wasn't looking forward to this. He looked at Rane's house again. Fucking werewolves! His family was becoming overrun by animals. His baby sister, who before all of this was shy and quiet, and he had to admit a pushover, was now mated to a werewolf and using her powers to help save the world. She was out of her shy shell, way out. He admitted to himself that he was proud of her, and he supposed that if she had to marry, or mate, or whatever the fuck they called it, at least it was someone he kind of liked and respected.

Logan walked toward his parents, moving slowly so he didn't freak them out with his battered and bruised body. His mother hugged him and he gritted his teeth to keep from wincing in pain. His dad nodded, but even his dad couldn't stop looking at the werewolves.

Logan's gaze fell on his brother, and he frowned. Hayden, who had been in worse condition than him, was walking around today looking like he hadn't almost died. Logan glanced at the hot, tall blonde smiling and basically eating his brother up.

Logan shook his head thinking, *God, us humans are*

idiots. How could we not have figured out that werewolves existed? A group of over two hundred ridiculously good looking people living together should bring attention to themselves. He was jolted out of his musing when Rane let slip that Kirby was pregnant, and in a little over six months there would be a new addition.

He blamed it on the pain that he was still in when he said, "What! We can breed with animals?"

Rane growled, and so did the hot blonde.

His mother gasped at him and he winced when she used his full name. "Logan Jonathan Brown, I did not bring you up to be like this."

He sighed and looked over to his brother for back up, and was shocked to see him glaring at him with a look of disappointment.

Logan turned back to his mother. "You can't tell me you're happy that your only daughter is married-mated to a werewolf, a being that turns into an animal?"

His mother's face was red as she turned to Rane, then the hot blonde. "I'm so sorry." She then turned back to Logan and whacked him upside the head. "These...beings, keep us safe, they have from the beginning of time, and I wouldn't care who my daughter..." She turned to Hayden. "...or son chose, as long as they are happy."

He looked to his brother again, who always had his back, but today he had his arm around the blonde. Hayden was looking at the blonde the same way she was looking at him.

"No, no, not you too. Fuck this!" Logan turned and walked out the door.

About Hazel Gower

I'm a mother of four terrors between the ages of two and seven. I started writing down my story ideas in high school, and never really stopped. Writing, I have to say, is my salvation. After I've cleaned up and gotten all the kids in bed, I sit at my computer—or sometimes a notebook with a pencil—and relax, write, and escape.

I love to hear from any of my readers, so feel free to send me an email and 'like' me on Facebook.

Hazel's Website:

www.hazelgower.com

Reader eMail:

hazel.gower@yahoo.com.au

About the Armageddon Mates Series

Book 1: *Kane's Mate*

Now Available

Book 2: *Rane's Mate*

Now Available

Book 3: *Ava's Mate*

Now Available